THE HEARTBREAK KID

ONE PASS AWAY: A NEW SEASON

BOOK FOUR

<u>DEDICATION</u>

To all the friends, lovers, and everyone in between.
Never give up on your dreams.

ABOUT THE AUTHOR

Writing isn't easy. But I love every second. A blank screen isn't the enemy. It is an opportunity to create new friends and take them on amazing adventures and life-changing journeys. I feel blessed to spend my days weaving tales that are unique—because I made them.

Billionaires. Songwriters. Artists. Actors. Directors. Stuntmen. Football players. They fill the pages and become dear friends I hope you will want to revisit again and again.

Thank you for jumping into my books and coming along for the journey.

HOW TO GET IN TOUCH

Please visit me at these sites, sign up for the Mary J. Williams newsletter, or leave a message.

Bookbub
Newsletter
Facebook
Twitter
Pinterest
Instagram
Goodreads

MORE BOOKS BY MARY J. WILLIAMS

AUDIOBOOKS

TABLE OF CONTENTS

PROLOGUE

FINNEGAN LLOYD LENNOX was thirteen years old.

Finn's age was nothing to brag about. He was average in the way of most teenage boys. He liked video games, pizza, and superhero movies. Most days, he hung out with his friends, who as with him, were typical examples of adolescent males. They argued. They laughed. They made rude noises—the louder the better.

And, most recently, something had changed. Finn, in the throes of full-blown, growth spurt inducing, hormone raging puberty, started to notice girls.

In his case, he couldn't keep his eyes from straying to one incredibly special, stand out from the crowd, girl.

No, Finn corrected himself. Not a *girl*. A *woman*.

At eighteen, she was beautiful, and smart, and sophisticated—at least in his less than experienced opinion. She was also so far out of his romantic league, he dared not hint to anyone of his new, sometimes exciting, often painful feelings.

If they knew the way Finn pined, his friends would take every opportunity to make his life a living hell. He could take the ribbing. Part of being a teenager was figuring out how to deal with the kind of verbal harassment only those closest to you could provide.

If the teasing got too out of hand, Finn could always punch someone in the face to shut him up. After all, knocking the crap out of your friends now and then was one of the joys of being a teenager.

Finn didn't give a rat's hind end what his friends had to say in private. However, if the truth of his feelings ever became public knowledge, if Erin Ashmore, the object of his affections, ever learned that just the thought of her could make his heart pound so hard he sometimes wondered how the vital organ managed to stay in his chest, his life was over.

Why? Because, quite simply, Erin would kill him.

Finn and Erin were an unlikely pair and had been from the moment they met the day she came to his house as a substitute babysitter. Certain he was too mature—too self-sufficient—to need someone to look after him, neither the word baby nor sitter sat well.

Put the words together—*babysitter*—and he, all of ten years old and filled with self-righteous resentment, was not a happy camper.

To say Finn and Erin's relationship started on a low note was an understatement. He was smart beyond his years. She, at the tender age of fifteen, possessed a stubborn streak a mile wide.

An only child of a widowed father, Finn had been coddled, protected, and indulged his entire life—until a blonde force of nature burst into his life. Unlike every adult he knew, Erin didn't fold up her tent and go home when his chin quivered, and tears filled his eyes. She didn't panic when he threw a conniption fit a mile wide and twice as long.

From the beginning, Erin Ashmore wasn't the least bit impressed with Finn or his whiny ways. And from day one, she wasn't afraid to let him know.

An immovable object bursting with energy, Erin was like no one Finn had encountered in his short life. When she put her mind to something, heaven help the fool who decided to stand in her way. He soon learned that she came by the nickname dozer—as in bull—honestly.

Through some subtle cajoling, a bit of trickery, and the kind of strategic thinking that even the most seasoned general would envy, Erin took an insular, spoiled rotten, overweight, *Cheetos* eating couch potato and transformed him into a healthy, active, outgoing boy.

2

The journey wasn't easy. Both suffered a few bruises and hurt feelings along the way. They argued, kicked, and screamed—literally and figuratively—and sometimes refused to speak to each other for days on end.

Somehow, three years later, they were best friends. The evolution in their relationship had been an epic battle—Erin's words and apt, Finn thought. He considered her to be a private miracle all his own.

Somehow, someway, Finn and Erin discovered they weren't so different after all. When they stopped barking and growling like a couple of junkyard dogs and began to communicate in full, reasonably modulated sentences, they clicked together like the final two missing pieces of a puzzle.

To say Finn and Erin completed each other was too corny and too simple an explanation. On paper, they never should have worked. But, thankfully for him, people didn't live their lives on paper.

Finn couldn't say when his feelings changed from friendship to something more. When did he realize that Erin smelled so good? Like a meadow of spring flowers mixed with honey and lemon. Why did just the brush of her hand suddenly send a shiver of awareness across his skin when before he never gave her touch a second thought?

As he lay awake at night, Finn pondered the moment he first noticed the softness of Erin's skin or the way her body curved in the most interesting places.

When? Finn couldn't say. All he knew was that something between them had changed and the feelings—bright, new, and confusing—were all on his side. Erin, thankfully, had no idea

For now, Finn was content to keep his feelings to himself. One day, when they were older—when he could face her as an equal in every way, he would confess. He had time.

Most of all, Finn was filled with the conviction his feelings would never change. Not tomorrow. Not in a million years.

Though often at a loss at how to deal with the emotions pinging and ponging through his body, Finn knew one thing with total certainty. If he wanted to keep Erin in his life and continue to hold her close as his best friend, she could never, ever, under any circumstances, find out how much he wanted his first kiss—his first everything—to be with her.

Luckily, for Finn and his budding libido, Erin had a way of pissing him off—thoroughly and frequently. If he was angry, like now, he almost forgot she was a woman. When she ranted, raved, and told him what to do, she became mercifully less appealing. For a brief, shining moment, his crush dimmed from a hard boil to a manageable simmer.

"No. Absolutely not." Erin stopped her pacing long enough to waggle a warning finger in Finn's face. "Do you hear me, Finnegan?"

Erin never used his full name unless she wanted to make a point. Or tease him. Or laugh at him. Hell, she used his full name all the time. A fact Finn added to the growing list of her annoying habits.

Unfortunately, when Erin called him Finnegan, she was cute. Truth be told, she was cute twenty-four hours a day, seven days a week. Finn stifled a sigh as he felt his temper cool and his hormones heat up. Even her faults made his blood race.

Cursing his misfortune under his breath, Finn realized—not for the first time—that he and his heart were royally screwed.

"Erin." Finn ran a hand through his shaggy red hair and sighed. Any attempt to stem the tide of her rising ire was a waste of time. But now and then, a man had to persevere even when he knew his mission was hopeless. "Take a breath. Now count to ten and remember. I want to play football, not jump off the *Empire State Building*."

As she resumed pacing—or stomping—down the corridor Erin stopped when she reached the end of the hallway. Amazed to find that anything, even the side of the building, had the nerve to block her path, her hand formed a fist.

"Don't hit the wall," Finn warned. "Short of turning into the *Hulk*, even you can't win a war against five reinforced inches of solid concrete. The school gymnasium was built to outlast even the wrath of Hurricane Erin."

Though never one to admit defeat, Erin wasn't a fool. Besides, she planned to be a doctor. The last thing she needed was to injure her hand in a losing battle. With a resigned huff, she turned on the heel of one bright red high-top *Keds*. Her long legs ate up the distance between them in record time.

When a scant foot of linoleum covered floor separated them, Erin stopped, crossed her arms, tipped her head to meet his gaze, and glared.

"Jump off a skyscraper? Play football? What's the difference? One way or another, both will kill you."

"Wow!" Finn scoffed. "When you exaggerate, you don't hold back. How can you compare playing an organized, school-sanctioned sport to me plummeting over one hundred stories before hitting the sidewalk with a splat?"

Logically, Finn knew he had Erin painted into a corner of her own making. Her argument didn't hold water against his. However, he forgot something he knew too well. She didn't understand the concept of failure. If she couldn't bulldoze her way with physical strength, her oh so nimble mind almost always found another way to secure victory.

"Which is better?" Erin asked with a smug smirk Finn recognized and didn't like. "A fast fall followed by fairly painless death? Or a slow march toward your mortality as you suffer from ruined joints, crippling pain, and a brain scrambled by multiple concussions?"

The way she painted a gruesomely graphic picture, Finn wondered why she didn't abandon the thought of a career in medicine and become a writer. He wasn't immune to the images she presented, but he refused to let her scare him into changing his mind.

"I want to try out for the team," Finn muttered. "Chances are I won't make the cut."

"Don't try and placate me," Erin said, a blue fire burning bright in her eyes. "The coach noticed the way you sprouted up over the school year and how you work out in your spare time. How many six foot-three-inch bodies with rapidly developing muscles and not an inch of extra fat does he have at his disposal?"

Still getting used to the changes in his body, Finn found himself caught between teenage embarrassment over the way Erin looked him over with a clinical eye and manly pride that she noticed how hard he worked at his physical transformation.

"The man must have drooled like a hungry dog presented with fresh meat," she sneered.

"Drooled? Fresh meat? Do you need to make it sound dirty?" Finn shuddered and wondered how he'd manage to look Coach Boseman—the least predatory man in the history of sports—in the eye without blushing.

"If tossing your mind in the gutter keeps you away from football, I'm fine with that," Erin said with an all too smug shrug.

"Nothing you said changed a thing," Finn told her, feeling a bit smug himself when her eyes widened in surprise.

Erin frowned as though confused by his stubborn attitude. Finn understood. From the moment she coaxed, wheedled, and shoved him out of his ten years of sedentary existence, she continued to run roughshod over his every major decision—and most of the minor ones.

Finn didn't consider himself a pushover. Instead, he spent the past three years in awe of Erin. Before she became his friend—and after—she was his hero. His savior. Despite her flaws—he wasn't foolish enough to believe she was perfect—he worshipped the ground on which she walked.

How could Finn *not* follow Erin's lead? By force then friendship, she changed the trajectory of his life and in the process, opened his eyes to a world of infinite possibilities. Including football.

Naturally, Erin assumed she would always have her way. She always did. However, she was about to discover that her influence ran deep. Along with a healthy lifestyle, she instilled Finn with a backbone and a strong sense of himself. Because his ideas for the future always ran parallel with hers, he had no reason to argue. Until now.

"I don't know what will happen," Finn told her. "But I'm excited to find out. More excited than I've been about anything in a long time."

Except for the idea of kissing you. Wisely, out of habit, Finn kept the last part to himself.

"I know you're smarter than the average thirteen-year-old." Erin's dry laughter held a smattering of humor—a fact Finn found encouraging. "However, though your brain allowed you to skip a grade and your body is bigger and stronger than most of your peers, you're still a boy who's barely started puberty."

The last thing Finn wanted or needed was Erin's reminder of his age—not when more than anything, he wished she would forget. If only for a day, or two, or three. Why couldn't she, just once, stop thinking of him as a *boy*.

Finn felt like a man, damn it. Especially when Erin was near.

Erin ran a hand down his arm before she stopped to squeeze his bicep. Finn's pulse jumped. While her touch was like fire, her smile held nothing but innocent intentions. With a less than pure mind, his body reacted in a *very* grownup manner.

Unaware of the slew of hormones unleashed by her fingers, Erin's tone was matter of fact. The pounding of his heart filling his ears, Finn tried to concentrate on her words, not her lingering hand.

"Under your impressive muscles are bones," Erin explained in her best, *I'll be a doctor one day*, tone of voice. "Bones break. They crack and crunch and crumble."

"Crumble?" Deliberately, Finn removed Erin's hand and moved three paces back until the wall stopped his retreat. As a form of protection, he curled his lip and adopted a surly tone. "What am I? Eighty with a severe case of osteoporosis?"

"Make all the jokes you like." Erin poked Finn's chest to emphasize each word. "I refuse to let you play football."

Finn prepared himself for Erin's protests. The reason he arranged to meet with her in the empty gymnasium was so she could vent, rage, and rail without witnesses. He listened, appreciated the points she made and was grateful for her concern.

And then, Finn did what Erin taught him to do by words and example. He held his ground.

"Like I said, making the team isn't a given." Finn knew his chances were good, but he saw no reason to share his confidence with Erin. "However, if I do, this fall, I *will* play football."

"You'll need your father's consent. After your mother died, he was so worried something might happen if you so much as received a paper cut, he practically wrapped you in cotton wool," Erin reminded him, grasping at her last straw. "Let his precious baby anywhere near a football field? I don't think so."

Lately, his son's wellbeing took a backseat to Jerry Lennox's bigger, more pressing problems. *Like how to pay off his ever-growing gambling debts.* A shadow flashed through Erin's expressive blue eyes telling Finn the moment she remembered why his father wasn't around very much these days.

Blessed with a loving mother and doting father, Erin's life wasn't all sunshine and roses, but she had the closest thing to a picture-perfect family as Finn could imagine. Sometimes he envied her. Mostly, he was simply grateful. He knew how much crap life could throw and the last thing he wanted was for Erin to go through the same hardships he'd encountered. If she was happy, so was he.

"All I need is an adult family member," Finn explained. "My mother's sister agreed to sign the consent form."

"Aunt Sheila," Erin muttered. "If I didn't like her so much, I'd give her an earful."

Finn hid his smile. Of all the people in the world, his aunt was the only one who could give his best friend a run for her money in the stubborn department. Erin wasn't intimidated. However, she maintained a healthy respect for Sheila Almont. Enough to wonder if push ever came to shove, which of them would win in a tussle of wills.

"I guess my days of influencing your decisions are over." Erin released a dramatic sigh. "Looks like my Finny went and became a man when I wasn't looking."

Damn straight, Finn thought, his chest puffing out with pride. *And about time you noticed.* Not that he expected anything to change. But at least he'd jumped on the right track toward someday holding Erin in his arms—man to woman.

"Don't think just because you won this once that I won't keep an eye on you, Finnegan Lennox." Erin smiled. "Even though I start college in the fall, and we won't see each other every day, I'll be royally pissed if you don't call me at least twice a week. Understand?"

As with everything else about Erin, the stubborn set of her chin made Finn's heart skip a beat. Along with the affirmation that she planned—insisted—on maintaining their close bond, he practically melted into a pool of adolescent goo.

"No reason you can't call me," Finn said, then added, "At least twice a week."

"Two calls from you, two from me?" Pausing, Erin raised an eyebrow. "Really?"

"Sounds good to me."

"And I thought we were already borderline codependent." With a laugh, she shrugged. "Why not?"

"Promise?" he asked. At the prospect of losing her, Finn suddenly felt less like the man he professed to be and more like a scared thirteen-year-old boy.

"Have I ever lied to you?" Erin demanded.

"All the time," Finn answered without hesitation.

"White lies don't count."

Finn snorted. Erin had a moral code all her own. Luckily for their friendship, her lies were never malicious. She might skew the truth from time to time, but always in aid of someone else and never for personal gain.

"Let me rephrase," Erin sighed, her blue eyes twinkling with amusement. "Have I ever gone back on a promise?"

"Never," Finn said. Erin's word, once given, was golden. "Not once."

"I don't plan to start," she told him. "But let's make one thing clear. I won't come to any of your games."

"Erin…"

"Non-negotiable, Finn." Erin shuddered. "I refuse to watch you purposely subject yourself to a beating. The best way to preserve our friendship is to not ask. Understood?"

"Let's make a deal." Finn's gray eyes narrowed as his brain plotted out a compromise. "If I turn out to have some talent and one day I play in the NFL? When my team makes it to the Super Bowl? You'll be there."

"What are the chances any of those things will happen?" Erin asked with a doubtful smile.

"Slim to none," Finn told her.

"I like the odds." Erin took his hand in hers and gave a firm shake. "Deal. On the day you play in the Super Bowl, I'll be there— come hell or high water."

"Since you never break a promise, I won't ask to get our agreement in writing."

"Gee, thanks." Erin laughed. "Where are you going?"

"Hold on a second," Finn said as he disappeared into the equipment room and found the item he stashed there earlier in the day.

Suddenly, Finn felt shy as he held out his gift. Erin's lips slowly curled upward. Her blue eyes glistened with what he thought might be an unshed tear.

"No one's ever given me flowers," she said, accepting the tentatively presented bouquet.

"Never?"

When Erin shook her head, her smile widening, Finn felt a wave of pride and accomplishment—as though he just crested the peak of Mount Everest.

"Why now?" she asked as she tentatively touched one petal.

"How often do you graduate from high school?" Finn said, answering her question with a question.

"Just once." Erin met his gaze with a worried frown. "You don't have the money to throw away on frivolous gifts."

"Frivolous?" Finn scoffed. "What kind of friend would I be if I let a major milestone in your life pass without getting you something? Should I give them to someone else?"

Erin pulled the flowers close to her chest; a protective reflex designed to keep Finn's grasp at bay but at the same time let the precious flowers remain unharmed.

"Give them to who?" she demanded. "I'm the only girl you know."

"I know plenty. And they flirt with me. Constantly," Finn told her. "Just need to decide which one I prefer."

"You don't know anything about the opposite sex." Erin frowned. "Guess we need to discuss the dangers of falling prey to a flirting girl at another time."

When Erin used the word discuss, she meant he was expected to listen while she did all the talking.

"When," Finn asked, wary of her answer.

"Later."

A threat or a promise. Finn couldn't decide.

"Much later," he said.

"We'll see. Right now, I want to enjoy my flowers." Erin did a little happy dance. "Any reason you chose red tulips?"

"The florist gave me a good deal," Finn said with a shrug.

A bald-faced lie, he thought as they walked from the gymnasium, but one Finn felt justified in telling. When he decided to buy Erin's gift, he researched his choice carefully. Different flowers held different meanings.

Tulips symbolized many things, depending on the color.

Yellow petals meant hope. White represented a new start. But Finn went with red for one simple reason. They were his only way of telling Erin without words what was in his heart.

Walking beside her, Finn thought about how he had changed since they met and how much was about to change. He thought about the future, the unknown.

Finn's gaze lingered on Erin's bright, beautiful face before his eyes lowered to the bouquet she held in her hands and smiled. She had no way of knowing.

Maybe one day he would tell her.

Red tulips. A declaration of true love.

CHAPTER ONE

"YOUR TABLE IS ready, Dr. Ashmore. Please follow me."

Erin smiled at the maître d´, nodding her head for him to lead the way. *Crescent Moon* was the hottest restaurant in Seattle. Consisting of only ten tables, the space was small, intimate, and elegant.

Booking a reservation at *Crescent Moon* was easy—if you didn't mind waiting two months. If Erin Ashmore called the front desk, she would have been relegated to the waitlist like everyone else. Lucky for her, she wasn't the average woman on the street. She was a doctor.

After years of studying, weeks on end with little sleep, and accrued student loans that rivaled the debt of a small nation, didn't she deserve a few perks? She didn't exploit her status often, but when the occasion arose—like today—she enjoyed her meal with a clear conscience.

Seated at the most requested table near the room's lone window, Erin ordered a bottle of her favorite Chablis. With a slight bow, the maître d´ nodded.

"Would you like me to have your waiter bring the wine right away, Dr. Ashmore?" he asked.

"I'll wait until my guest arrives, Carl," Erin answered as she looked at the man's smiling face, a sparkle in her blue eyes. "How are you and your wife enjoying the new grandbaby?"

"Scarlett is our little angel." Carl let out a contented sigh. "We'll never be able to thank you enough for making sure she came into the world. We worried our daughter might miscarry. You performed a miracle."

"All I did was prescribe a course of action. Trisha did all the work," Erin assured him. "Because she was diligent and followed my instructions to the letter, she was able to carry her beautiful, healthy baby girl to term."

"Don't try to dismiss the role you played," Carl told her. "Most doctors don't check up on their patients as often as you. Nor do they personally deliver packages filled with nutritious food and gossip magazines."

Erin felt a tickle of embarrassment. She possessed a healthy ego—most doctors did. And she wasn't averse to accepting the odd compliment or two. However, when a patient or her loved one gushed over what she considered the basics of her job, she wanted nothing more than to change the subject and move on.

As if sensing Erin's discomfort, Carl gave her another bow before leaving her alone to peruse the menu. Everything sounded delicious. Whenever possible, the chef sourced ingredients from local farmers and fishermen. As a result, eating the food at *Crescent Moon* was a true Pacific Northwest experience.

"Am I late?"

Erin looked up as Riley Preston slid into the chair opposite hers.

"I'm early," Erin said. She looked at her watch. "You, as always, are right on time."

"You sound annoyed." Riley laughed.

"Just once, I'd like you to be bad at something," Erin sighed. "Remind me why we're friends again?"

"Beats me." Riley shrugged. "Lord knows we hated each other when we were younger."

"Hate is a strong word," Erin said, her mind drifting back to when they attended the same high school.

"Strongly disliked?" Riley asked with a quizzical expression. "Though I can't for the life of me understand why you thought of me one way or the other. You were pretty and popular. I was quiet and dull as a mouse."

Riley's description of her teenage self was accurate. But times had changed. Gone was the girl who wore baggy clothes and tried her best to fade into the woodwork. At thirty-six, she was beautiful, successful, wickedly smart, and one of the most fashion-forward women in Seattle. The only person who equaled the businesswoman's love of designer labels was Erin.

"We're friends because you changed," Riley said.

"Me?" Erin scoffed. "I don't think so."

When Riley remained silent, her gaze steady, Erin frowned as she considered the possibility. She always thought Riley was the one who transformed herself. But no one stayed the same, even if the changes were incremental.

As Riley decided on what to choose from the menu, Erin mentally took a brief trip back in time.

Though they grew up in the same city and attended the same school, for the first twenty-five years of their lives, no one would have called Erin and Riley friends. Yet, they didn't socialize or interact enough to be called enemies or rivals.

Wouldn't they have been surprised to learn how much they were envied by the other?

Teenage Riley was painfully shy. Erin, bold and outgoing. The Preston family was rich. The Ashmore clan lived from paycheck to paycheck. If asked, the girls would have sworn the other had a perfect life.

Years later, Erin realized she was the lucky one. Unlike Riley whose parents were the definition of a horror show, she grew up loved and cared for. Money, she discovered, could buy many things, but happiness wasn't one of them.

"I could never understand why you looked so miserable," Erin said with an aching heart. "You have no idea how much I wanted to be you. If just for a day."

"I felt the same." Riley laughed at herself—a useful ability she didn't possess when she was younger. "Times change, thank goodness. Now, I wouldn't trade my life for anything."

"Why would you?" Erin snorted. "You have more money than God. The football team you inherited are Super Bowl champions. Best of all, your husband is too sexy for words *and* worships the ground you walk on."

"Everyone should marry the love of her life," Riley agreed. Her blue eyes, a shade lighter than Erin's, narrowed thoughtfully. "Would you still swap lives with me if given the chance? Even for one day?"

"No." Erin didn't have to think twice. "First, as gorgeous as he is, the idea of kissing Sean is plain weird. No offense."

"Women have drooled over Sean McBride for most of his life." Riley let out a resigned sigh. "One less—especially a close friend—is a bit of a relief."

"Your fault," Erin teased. "You should have loved a less attractive man."

"Trouble is, I fell early and hard." Riley shook her head. "I tried my best to change my heart. I tried other men. For worse, then better, Sean was always the one."

"Which is a big reason why I don't want your life," Erin said. "Between my private practice and the three days a week I work at *Seattle General Hospital*, I barely have time to squeeze in a yoga class. What would I do with a husband?"

"When you meet the right man, the answer to your question will fall in your lap," Riley told her.

"*When* I meet the right man, not *if?*" Erin asked, uncertain if she admired the certainty of Riley's words or resented them. "I'm thirty-five years old—"

"Thirty-six," Riley interrupted, grinning when Erin's eyes narrowed.

Erin didn't worry about the passage of time. If she was healthy and her mind was sound, age didn't matter. One year was pretty much like the next. However, she saw no reason to skip ahead a month all willy-nilly. Time passed quickly enough without any help from her—or her friend.

"My point is," Erin said to a still smiling Riley. "Sharing my body with a man is one thing; giving my heart is another story. Brief, satisfying sexual flings are all I need or want."

"I could argue. But I won't." Riley placed her order. "Instead, tell me why you invited me to lunch."

"I'll have the salmon," Erin told the waiter, then turned to Riley. "Would you like some wine while we wait for our food? Or do you need to get back to the office?"

"My schedule is pretty light this week," Riley said. She took a sip of the crisp white Chablis and let out a sigh of pleasure. When Erin casually crossed her legs, her lips curved into a smile. "Now I know why I'm here. You wanted to show off your shoes."

Glancing at her feet, Erin realized the toe of one honey-colored pump pointed in Riley's direction as if to say, *look at me*. She laughed.

Suppressing a smug smile, Erin rotated her ankle in a slow circle. The shoes just hit the market. The fact that she snatched up a pair before her friend put a check on her side of the ledger in their ongoing game of fashionista one-upmanship. Her satisfaction lasted just long enough for Riley to set a croc-embossed purse on the table.

"Unfair," Erin cried in frustration. "You know I had my eye on the new *Rebecca Lawrence* satchel. How did you manage to get one already?"

"Talent," Riley bragged. "Plus, Sean used his Hollywood connections to pull a few strings."

"I call foul." Erin ran a covetous gaze over the pale lavender bag. "Rebecca Lawrence is married to a movie star. Sean co-starred with her husband in an action flick. Talk about an inside job. How am I supposed to compete?"

"Last month you used one of your grateful patients to procure the *Ralph Lauren* dove gray bomber jacket I wanted more than my next breath," Riley reminded her. "I'd say, for now, we're even. Wouldn't you?"

"For now," she conceded reluctantly.

Erin took a sip of wine as she gathered her thoughts. Riley was right. She did have an ulterior motive for asking her friend to lunch—a reason that had nothing to do with exclusive designer one-upmanship.

However, now that the moment was at hand, Erin felt oddly reluctant to broach the subject straight out. The topic of fashion seemed a good segue into her true motivation.

"Did I ever tell you how I acquired my first pair of shoes that didn't come off the rack?" Erin asked.

"No." Riley shook her head. "I'm sure I'd remember."

"Finn," Erin said.

"Finn Lennox?" Riley laughed when Erin nodded. "He *is* the most stylish man I know. However, I would have bet a bundle that you were the one who taught him how to rock a suit."

"I'd love to take credit, but Finn's fashion sense is all his own." Erin smiled. "After college, when he signed his first professional contract, he gave me a pair of *Manolo Blahnik* boots to celebrate."

"Nice," Riley said, obviously impressed.

"To say I was shocked by the gift would be a major understatement." Erin shook her head at the memory. "Appalled might be a better word."

"Why?" Riley's eyes widened. "You love pretty things."

"I do now," Erin agreed. "Back then, I was a cash-strapped intern who needed to share a one-bedroom apartment with three equally impoverished doctors just to make rent each month."

"Now I feel guilty," Riley said.

"Because you had a trust fund to fall back on?" Erin shrugged off the thought. "You paid the price with crappy parents."

"True." Riley sighed as a brief shadow darkened her normally bright blue eyes. Just as quickly, she blinked the darkness away. "Finish your story. I'm intrigued. What did you say when Finn presented you with a pair of pricy boots?"

"I told him I'd rather have the money." Erin winced.

"Ouch," Riley said in sympathy.

"Mm. Not my finest moment," Erin agreed. "For the first time in his life, he was able to give me something nice and I ruined the moment. You should have seen the look in his eyes. I felt as though I'd kicked a puppy."

"I don't need you to tell me that Finn, and his expensive taste in clothes, survived the blow," Riley said with a sympathetic smile.

"Oh, yes." Erin laughed. "Aided and abetted when he won rookie of the year and was rewarded with his first big endorsement deal—for an *incredibly* famous fashion house. He bought a house just so he'd have space for his growing wardrobe."

"I can relate." Riley winked. "But what about the *Manolo Blahniks*? Did you keep the boots?"

"Of course," Erin said. "Would you believe I still have them? They occupy a place of honor in my closet—next to the shoes purchased once *I* started to earn a living."

"I love a happy ending." Riley took a bite of her butter braised pork loin. She sighed with pleasure. "Yum."

Erin enjoyed her meal, waiting patiently until Riley was sated with food and wine before she revealed her true motives.

"Are you aware that Finn is a free agent?" she asked in as casual a manner as possible.

"Finn is the best wide receiver in the NFL. Everyone who follows football knows his status." Riley paused, her fork halfway to her mouth. With a knowing smile, she slowly set the utensil onto her plate. "*Now* I understand. The food? The wine? The heart-tugging shoe story? All a diversion."

"I don't know what you mean," Erin said with an innocent expression—or as innocent as she could manage.

"Don't play coy with me, missy," Riley scoffed. "You want to know if the *Knights* plan to make Finn an offer."

Erin saw no advantage in keeping up the pretense. Riley was right, she did want information. And why not? After all her friend owned the team.

"You said yourself that Finn is the best." Erin felt a burst of pride. "The Knights would be crazy not to snap him up before another team beats them to the punch."

"Maybe." Riley shrugged as she picked up her fork. "I'm not the person to ask about personnel moves."

"The Seattle Knights belong to you," Erin argued.

"I'm the majority owner," Riley agreed. "However, the decision on which players the team signs rests with our general manager and head coach. Not me."

"Bull-pucky," Erin scoffed.

"Working together—working their tails off—Darcy Stratham and Joshua McClain achieved what everyone said was an impossible feat. They led the *Knights* to the Super Bowl. They brought the championship back to Seattle," Riley said, practically glowing with happiness. "They've earned my trust. Whatever off-season moves they decide to make, I'm fully on board."

Erin believed her friend—up to a point. Riley Preston inherited a fortune from her grandfather. Unlike many rich kids, she wasn't content to live on interest payments and stock dividends. Ambitious, proud, she turned millions into billions.

Shrewd and diligent, Riley rarely let sentiment get in the way of business. The *Knights* organization, the team she loved from the time she was a little girl, was no different. Erin didn't doubt for a second that if Riley wanted someone to play for the *Knights*, she wouldn't hesitate to use the weight of her influence to get the player to sign on the dotted line.

Now, all Erin needed to do was to make Riley want Finn.

"He was born and raised in Seattle. Heck, the three of us attended the same high school."

"I remember," Riley said.

Certain she was on the right path, Erin pushed ahead.

"Finn and the *Knights* are a perfect fit. Just think of the headline." Erin pictured the bold print. *"**NFL Superstar Comes Home**."*

"Catchy," Riley agreed. "If you ever decide to give up your OB/GYN practice, give me a call. I'll find you a place in our publicity department."

"Funny," Erin muttered.

"Why the sudden interest in Finn's career path," Riley asked, turning serious. "This is his second time as a free agent. You didn't push me to sign him three years ago."

"Finn was happy in Chicago," Erin explained. "And I…"

"And what?" Riley asked with an encouraging smile.

"Finn and I have been best friends for twenty years." A whoosh of breath left Erin's lungs. "Wow. When I say the number aloud, I can't believe how much time has passed."

"He'll always be five years younger," Riley teased.

"A fact Finn likes to bring up whenever he wants to piss me off," Erin said, her smile rueful. "Did you know we shared an apartment in college? Not that we saw much of each other. When I wasn't in class, my job, and sporadic love life, kept me busy."

"University of Washington gave Finn a full scholarship, right?" Riley asked.

Erin hoped Finn would get football out of his system in high school. She was wrong. Turned out he was gifted with the kind of talent that only came around once in a generation—or so he was told

21

by the myriad of coaches who tried to convince him to play for their program.

Ultimately, though Finn could have gone anywhere in the country, he decided to stay at home.

"I was thrilled when Finn picked UW," Erin said. "I wouldn't trade the time we had together for anything. But when he was drafted by Chicago, he was worried we'd grow apart."

"What did *you* think?" Riley asked.

"I was certain the time apart would be good for him," Erin said. "Good for *us*."

"Were you right?"

Erin sighed, then smiled. To say they hadn't experienced a few growing pains would be a lie. Ultimately, she and Finn adapted to their long-distance friendship. If anything, rather than weakening, as they became independent adults, their bond strengthened.

"I have no regrets," Erin told Riley. "But eight years is long enough. It's time for Finn to come home."

"The decision is out of my hands," Riley reiterated. "You can talk to Darcy and Mac if you want. But they make their decisions with the good of the team in mind. Not to mention, the salary cap. Finn's asking for a lot of money—as he should. I'm just not sure his salary fits within the organization's budget."

Why, Erin lamented as she walked the six blocks between the restaurant and her apartment, did everything in life boil down to money? Even if the Knights wanted to sign Finn, his salary could put a kibosh on the deal. He deserved every dollar and though she wished he could move back to Seattle; she would never want him to cut his asking price just so she could see him every day.

Taking the elevator to the top floor, Erin tapped the code into the door's keypad. Once inside, she slipped off her shoes and padded across the hardwood floor. A bank of floor to ceiling windows covered one wall presenting a picture-perfect view of Puget Sound.

Leaning against the back of the sofa, Erin gazed at the expanse of water. The first time she walked into the apartment, she knew she was home. Two floors and a rooftop deck where she tested her gardening skills—she quickly learned her thumb was more brown than green—the place became her sanctuary.

Though Erin loved her job, she needed a quiet, peaceful space away from the pressures and demands of her daily life where she could unwind and let herself simply be.

For the first time since she moved in, Erin felt a wave of loneliness. Something was missing. No. Someone. She sighed.

"I miss you, Finn."

CHAPTER TWO

PHOTOSHOOTS WERE SECOND nature to Finn Lennox. He wouldn't say that standing in front of a camera came as naturally as breathing—or catching touchdown passes. However, he felt at ease under the studio lights. More often than not, he knew what to do well before the photographer uttered his or her instructions.

Posing for an advertising campaign wasn't rocket science, but there was a kind of art to selling a product. The angle of his body mattered. As did the way he smiled or if he simply let the intensity of his gray eyes tell the story.

After ten years and hundreds of product endorsement deals, Finn knew what worked and what didn't. The sponsors paid him an exorbitant fee for one simple reason. Because when he held a tube of toothpaste or stood next to a sleek sports car, he made them a lot of money.

Stepping out into the seasonably warm Chicago afternoon sun, Finn closed his eyes and lifted his face toward the light. Happy to take a break, he rolled his shoulders one way, then the other.

Finn had come a long way from the first time he stepped in front of a camera. Barely twenty-two years old, awkward as hell, unsure where to put his hands or his feet, he suffered through the three-hour photo shoot, sweating profusely and praying for the torture to end.

To Finn's surprise, everyone raved over the pictures calling him a natural. To his eyes, he looked constipated, but to each his own. If not for the hefty boost to his bank account, he never would have agreed to do the next endorsement. Or the next. Or the next.

As was almost always the case, money talked. At the time, Finn's dire financial status meant he was in no position to let his personal feelings get in the way.

Eventually, Finn learned to relax when the camera was on him to the point where he enjoyed getting his picture taken. And why not? With little effort on his part, he was fussed over and pampered. As a perk of the job, his closet was filled with the designer suits, shoes, and sportswear he modeled.

Yes, life was good for Finnegan Lennox. And if everything went according to his plan, things were about to get better. A *whole lot* better.

Taking his phone from his back pocket, Finn tapped the top name on his contact list. Three rings later, the face of his favorite person in the world filled the screen. Makeup free but for a touch of cherry-colored lip gloss and wearing a t-shirt that proclaimed her love of all things chocolate, Erin Ashmore was without qualification, a balm to his soul.

"Finn!" Erin exclaimed, her smile beaming. "I planned to call you later. Did your photoshoot end early?"

"Just taking a break," Finn told her. "I didn't expect to catch you at home. Glad you managed to get away from the clinic at a decent hour for once."

"Savoring the lull before the storm," Erin said with a laugh. "I have four expectant mothers on baby watch. Fingers crossed they don't all pop at the same time."

"Is pop a technical term?" Finn teased with a raised eyebrow.

"Yes, smartass." Erin stuck out her tongue. "Though I refrain from using the word in front of my patients. I don't like to plant the image of a bursting vagina in the head of a mother-to-be."

"I don't imagine the fathers react well either." Finn knew he wouldn't.

"Men," Erin scoffed. "They're all testosterone and bluster at first. But when I show them a video of live childbirth, they dissolve into masses of liquified jelly."

Finn chuckled. Erin felt every worry, pain, heartache, and joy experienced by her patients. Anyone else had to stand in line if he or she decided to whine or complain. Until the husband, boyfriend, or partner managed to switch places with the person tasked with carrying a baby, her sympathy had its limits.

"Speaking for my male brethren," Finn began.

"Yes?" Erin moved her face close to the phone so Finn couldn't miss the warning signals in her blue eyes. "If you want to defend your half of the species, be my guest."

Biting back a grin, Finn quickly and wisely forgot whatever nonsense he might have blabbered in a moment of temporary insanity. Instead, he focused on Erin. An easy assignment, as always.

"You cut your hair."

Though Erin wasn't fooled for a second by Finn's attempt to divert her attention, she did what any best friend would do. She allowed his brief lapse in judgment to pass without another comment.

"I had a few inches trimmed off," she said as she touched the ends of her bobbed, shoulder-length hair. "The change isn't drastic. Fact is, you're the only person who's noticed."

The reason was simple, Finn thought. He noticed everything about Erin because everything about her mattered to him. As a doctor, her patients relied on her to stay calm, cool and collected. To do her job, she learned to curb her naturally effusive personality.

Erin could hide her emotions from others, but not from Finn. One look and he knew when she was happy, or sad, or hurt. Twenty years of friendship gave him an advantage. The fact that he'd loved her almost as long was his ace in the hole. She could put on a brave face, but he saw past the mask—every time.

Today all Finn saw when he looked into Erin's blue eyes was a burst of joy. Squinting into the sun, he smiled. When she was happy, the world just seemed a bit brighter.

"Speaking of hair," Erin said. "I thought you planned to cut yours and shave before the photoshoot."

Finn ran his fingers through the thick red hair that fell several inches past his shoulders before tugging on the ends of his full beard. Last fall, he and a few of his fellow teammates let both grow out on a whim—fueled by a beer, or two. One by one, pressured by girlfriends, wives, and mothers, his buddies broke down and returned to their original short hair, clean-shaven style. Nine months later, out of stubbornness, he was the only mountain man left standing—so to speak.

The fact that Erin expressed a fondness for his shaggier persona didn't hurt his decision not to make his usual scheduled visit to his favorite salon.

"You said the unkempt look suited me," Finn reminded her.

"Did I?" Erin asked, lips twitching.

Finn nodded. He remembered because she commented on how soft his beard felt when he hugged her goodbye after he visited Seattle a few months earlier.

"That was then," Erin told him. "Lately, I miss seeing your pretty face. Besides, didn't the executive in charge of the campaign want more of a sexy, GQ look to the ads? Sleek, ungodly expensive watch. A slick, equally costly man sporting the timepiece on his wrist. Or some such nonsense."

"Mock if you like," Finn said. "My guess is you won't say no to the lady's watch I received as a thank you gift for my invaluable services."

"Goodies for me?" Erin perked up.

Finn nodded.

"Do whatever the sponsor asks," she told him.

Erin was so unabashedly materialistic; Finn couldn't help but grin. She loved nice things, a fact he understood very well since he felt the same. Yet, she didn't hesitate to donate her time and skills at three local women's shelters, not to mention the money she donated every year to the causes closest to her heart.

Few people knew of Erin's altruism because she didn't believe in advertising good deeds. Again, Finn felt the same. When he volunteered, the work he did was to benefit others, not stroke his ego.

"Right now, the sponsor wants before and after pictures. First, sexy lumberjack—her words, not mine. Then, after a shave and haircut, I'll represent the suave man about town." Finn grabbed the lapels of the jacket he would wear for the next set of pictures. "Not sure if a white silk jacket with no shirt exactly screams sophistication."

"The person in charge of the campaign is a woman?" When he nodded, Erin snickered. "I should have known. She wants to see your impressive chest—and knows everyone in the viewing audience agrees."

"Are you insinuating that a woman is incapable of setting aside personal feelings when on the job?" Finn made a tsking sound with his tongue. "Shame on you, Erin. Time to turn in your feminist card."

"I don't need a card," she told him. "Feminism is in my DNA."

Finn knew Erin's parents and admired them more than he could say. Her mother and father believed in letting their children shine in whatever way made them happy—no matter their gender. To them, freedom of choice without judgment was the very definition of feminism.

"As for a woman in the workforce?" Erin continued. "You don't lose any points simply because you can admire a fine-looking man. Your lady executive sounds like one smart cookie. Women—and men—will admire shaggy Finn as well as sophisticated Finn."

"Think so?" Finn asked.

"Bottom line, her client, your boss, will sell *a lot* of watches."

"You missed your calling, Ms. Ashmore," Finn said with a wink. "You should have majored in advertising."

"Maybe you're right," Erin nodded, her expression thoughtful. "Just the other day, Riley offered me a job working for the Knights in the publicity department."

"Did she?" Finn laughed. "Riley's one of the smartest cookies I know. What did you do to earn her admiration?"

"A story for another time," Erin said with a wave of her hand. "Right now, I need to know if you decided where you plan to play football next season."

After Finn signed his rookie contract, Erin was resigned but not thrilled that he chose football as a career. Seven years ago, when he re-upped with Chicago, then accepted an extension year before last, she barely commented.

As Finn entered his second go-round as a free agent, Erin's attitude was different. She texted him daily, eager, and anxious to know what was going on. To be honest, he loved the attention.

Today, Finn's main reason for calling Erin was to share the latest information. He should have known that before he could broach the subject, Erin would beat him to the punch.

"I need your advice," he said. His tone was casual, but his heart pounded hard in his chest.

"Advice is my forte," Erin said. Her gaze narrowed. "Not that you listen to me the way you once did."

"Wrong. I hear everything you say," Finn corrected. "The difference is, unlike when I was a wet behind the ears kid in awe of every move you made, I'm now an adult. Be honest. You would be appalled if I relied on you to tell me every move I should make."

"Well…" Erin shrugged, unwilling to admit he was right.

If I consulted you every time my backside needed wiping, how long would our friendship have lasted?"

"About three seconds," Erin admitted.

"There you go." Finn sighed. "You pretend to be a control freak, but where other people are concerned, the last thing you want is to micromanage their lives."

"First, you're right." Erin shuddered at the idea. "Second, you aren't now, nor have you ever been, *other* people. You're my Finn. And though I disagree about micromanaging, I still want—*need*— to have a say. Even if you ignore every word I say."

Finn lost track of what Erin had to say after she pretty much admitted that he belonged to her. She owned his heart—had for most of his life. If she said the word, he would gladly relinquish the rest of himself.

Okay, to be fair, Finn would hold onto his free-will with a firm grip. After all, he wasn't a masochist. But the rest? He was hers. Body and soul.

"I won't ignore you today," Finn said. "About my decision. Chicago made an offer."

Erin didn't answer right away but Finn could see her emotions play out over her expressive face in vivid technicolor. Worry. Annoyance. Anger. A bit of a pout. Then, at last, a cagey kind of determination all her own.

"You love the city," she said with a shrug. "Why, I can't say. Too hot in the summer, balls-freezing cold in the winter. But hey, to each his own."

"Seattle is better?" Finn asked, knowing Erin would jump to her hometown's defense. "Rain. Cold. Wind. And did I mention the rain?"

"Annually in the United States, Seattle doesn't fall in the top ten. So, there." Erin stuck out her tongue.

Finn wanted to tell her how damn cute she was. Instead, his lip curled into a sneer.

"Very mature," he said. "The point is each city has a set of pros and cons. Since I received an offer from the *Bears* and the *Knights*, I—"

"What did you say?" Erin screeched as literally, she bounced out of the picture.

Patiently, enjoying the show, Finn waited while Erin ran around her living room, lapping her stationary phone three times before coming to a breathless halt in front of the screen.

"Tell me again," she demanded.

"Chicago—"

"I don't care about your old team," Erin interrupted. "Tell me about the *Knights*. Your *new* team."

"Don't get ahead of yourself," Finn warned. "I haven't made up my mind which of the contracts to sign."

"Is money the issue?" Her displeasure evident, Erin sighed. "Now I understand why Riley didn't tell me the Knights made you an offer when I asked. She lowballed you."

Finn opened his mouth to explain but before he could utter a word, Erin continued her rant against her friend.

"Riley is a shrewd businesswoman, but I never dreamed she was cheap," Erin hissed through clenched teeth. "She mentioned some nonsense about a salary cap. Just an excuse not to open the purse strings."

"The NFL mandated salary cap is a very real thing," Finn informed her. "Teams struggle every year as they figure out what player they can afford and which they have to let go."

"The *Knights* should dump the dead weight and grab onto you," she proclaimed. "Riley admitted—without any prompting on my part—that you're the best wide receiver in the league. Maybe the greatest. Period."

"I doubt she called me the best to play the game," Finn admonished. He appreciated Erin's loyalty, but even his ego stopped short of too much hyperbole.

"Fine," Erin admitted. "I *sensed* her opinion. When management is presented with the chance to bring the best to Seattle, shouldn't they make it happen? Crunch the numbers. Jump through a few hoops."

"Erin."

"Yes?"

"Breathe."

"Fine," Erin huffed. "I'll breathe."

Finn waited for a beat while she did as he instructed.

"The money offered by each team is about the same." He shrugged. "The perks and incentives are close—a little better on the Seattle side."

"Then what's the problem." Erin shook her phone as though holding him instead. "Sign, man. Sign!"

"I wanted to ask you first." Finn cleared his throat. Though he knew her answer, he suddenly felt a wave of nerves. "We haven't lived in the same city for almost a decade. "Are you sure you want me darkening your doorstep day and night?"

"Doorstep, my left foot," Erin scoffed. "You'll stay here, with me."

Exactly what he hoped she would say. Finn felt every muscle in his body relax. Still, he wasn't above playing hard to get.

"I don't know." Frowning, Finn rubbed the back of his neck. "Living together when we were in college was one thing. We were too busy to get on each other's nerves. But now..."

"We're still busy," Erin said. "The only change is our financial situations. Instead of a tiny, one-bedroom apartment with paper-thin walls and plumbing older than dirt, we get to live in luxury."

"The closet in the guest room isn't big enough to hold my shoes, let alone the rest of my clothes."

Finn knew he had his reluctance a step too far. But he never found himself in the position where Erin wanted something so much that she was practically ready to beg—or as close as she would ever come. Between her pleading and the earnest expression on her face, he couldn't resist pushing his luck a little further.

If Erin caught on to his ploy. If she lost her temper and hung up. No problem. Finn would call her back and apologize. She never took long to forgive him. She could never stay mad at him for long any more than he could hold his temper against her.

"The guest area was remodeled since the last time you stayed over." Erin frowned. "Didn't I mention that the contractor eliminated the third bedroom and expanded the second bathroom and closet?"

"Hm." Finn tapped his chin. Of course, he remembered. "If you're certain I'll have enough space. You know how I like my clothes to have room enough to breathe."

"They can breathe," Erin promised. "Heck, there's room for your shirts to jitterbug with your dress shoes if they're so inclined. The closet is now just as big as mine."

"Okay." Finn was through screwing around.

"Really?" Erin clapped her hands together. "You'll sign with Seattle?"

"I will," he nodded.

"And move in with me?"

"I'll start shipping my things *if* I pass my physical," Finn assured her.

"You'll pass," Erin said, unconcerned. "When will you get here?"

"Two weeks." Finn loved her enthusiasm, but he couldn't dismantle the life he'd built in Chicago overnight—even if he wanted to. "Three at the most."

"Fine." Erin sighed. "Warning, Finnegan. If you change your mind, I'll never forgive you."

"Make me a promise?" Finn asked.

"Maybe." Erin hated to commit her word unless she knew the details.

"Take care of yourself." Finn was dead serious. "If you get so much as a papercut before I arrive, *I'll* never forgive *you*."

"Yes, you will." Erin laughed. "But because I'm so happy, I'll do as you ask."

"Say the words," Finn urged.

"What are you, twelve?" Erin shook her head. "Fine. I promise to take care of myself. But what happens after you get here?"

"Simple," he said. "You won't need to worry because I'll be there."

"How can such a cool man manage to deliver such a cheesy line." Erin cringed. "The least you could do is blush."

"I'm too cool to blush." When Erin rolled her eyes, Finn chuckled. "Talk to you soon."

Smiling, Finn turned and ran smack dab into his agent. Arms crossed, Alvin Poe shook his head.

"I thought you were inside." Finn frowned. "How long were you standing there?"

"Long enough," Alvin told him. "Isn't Erin Ashmore your best friend?"

"Has been since we were kids," Finn said as they walked from the sunlight into the dimly lit photography studio. "Did the stylist I requested arrive to cut my hair?"

"And shave off the beard," Alvin assured him. "Karen is setting up her stuff in your dressing room."

"Good. I'd like to get out of here in time to watch the baseball game live instead of off the DVR." Finn slipped out of the silk jacket, handed the garment to the person in charge of his wardrobe, and accepted a plain black t-shirt in exchange. "Cubs versus Seattle. Funny, no?"

"Hilarious," Alvin muttered.

As his agent trailed behind him to the dressing room, Finn shot him a questioning look.

"By the deep furrow between your brows, I assume you have something on your mind."

"You signed the contract with the Knights this morning," Alvin said.

"True," Finn agreed with a nod. "So?"

"I heard you on the phone." Alvin shrugged. "Why did you tell your best friend that you hadn't made up your mind which team to choose?"

"Ah." Now, Finn understood the confusion. "Erin is never happier than when she has to fight for what she wants."

"So?" Alvin urged with a trace of impatience.

"She wanted to convince me. I wanted to let her." Finn didn't see anything strange in the arrangement. Alvin still seemed confused, but he wasn't in the mood to explain—even if he could. "Trust me when I say the dynamic between us has worked for twenty years."

"If it ain't broke, don't fix it?" Alvin asked.

"Close enough." Finn took a seat and let his favorite hairstylist tuck a protective cape around him. "All you need to know is, thanks to you and the generous contract you negotiated, I'm going home."

"Glad I could be of service." Alvin hesitated before leaving the room. "The way you bicker, the two of you seem more like siblings than friends."

"I'm not Erin's brother." Finn shot out words, emphasizing each one, and ending with a growl.

"Okay!" Alvin threw up his hands in surrender. "Just saying, the way you argue, something's going on besides friendship. Good luck with sharing the same house."

Alvin shut the door with a firm click before Finn could respond. Not that he had anything to say. For close to twenty years, he'd kept his feelings for Erin to himself. When he finally admitted the truth, it would be to her and no one else.

"Sexual tension," Karen said as she trimmed away the first layer of his beard.

"Pardon?" Finn asked.

"The reason you and Erin argue so much," she told him with a knowing smile. "Classic case of wanting what you can't have. Trouble is, you don't know how to break out of the friend zone. Am I right?"

Amused that Karen saw clearly what Alvin hadn't, Finn lowered one shoulder in a non-comital shrug.

"None of my business," the stylist said. "Just saying if you want her, the time to make your move is now. Consensual cohabitation can lead to some very sexy opportunities."

Finn's thoughts exactly. He'd waited a long time for Erin. Now was his time to act on the feelings he suppressed in deference to the relationship he believed she wanted.

The last time they lived together Finn was still a boy in so many ways. Now, he was all man—mentally and physically. Most of all, he and Erin were finally on equal footing.

Determined to make his intentions clear, Finn was ready to fight for what he wanted. Erin. Heart *and* body. He refused to settle for anything else.

CHAPTER THREE

FINN WASN'T AFRAID to fly. He appreciated the convenience of getting on a plane in one city and landing in another after only a few hours of airtime. If he drove from Chicago to Seattle, the trip would take over a day—if he didn't account for bathroom breaks or the need to refuel himself and his car.

As a professional athlete, Finn flew thousands of miles a year to away games then back home.

No, Finn wasn't afraid to get on a plane. However, he was only human. Though he understood the principles of flight, every time the massive metal machine lifted off the ground, he felt a sense of awe—and a niggling of doubt that something made of metal and weighed down with hundreds of human beings could remain airborne.

Finn wasn't particularly religious. Still, he didn't believe in tempting fate. Once the plane's wheels hit the ground again and the massive flying machine came to a complete halt, he always said a small, silent prayer of thanks.

Once Finn joined the NFL and money was no longer a pressing issue, he used his off-season time to unwind and reconnect with Erin. Together, they took a yearly, two-week vacation. Adventurous by nature, they enjoyed visiting foreign countries, exploring different cultures, sampling exotic cuisines.

A sunny beach one time, an alpine retreat the next. For Finn, the destination wasn't as important as the company. Without Erin, his innate curiosity about the world would have been impetus enough.

But, as with most things, traveling with her was a lot more fun than making the trip alone.

Today, as Finn left the plane and walked into the Seattle/Tacoma International Airport terminal, Erin wasn't his companion, she was his destination. Just the thought of seeing her beautiful face was enough to put a bounce in his step.

Finn wasn't a visitor. He wouldn't leave Erin behind after a few short days. He was home. As reality finally settled into his mind and his bones, he felt as though his body let out a giant sigh.

The only words Finn could think of to describe his feelings were *at last.*

Stopping, Finn stretched his arms over his head. When he felt a large, slightly sweaty body knock into his, he shook his head. He turned to find his agent dodging bodies and scrambling to pick his phone up off the ground before one of their fellow travelers crushed it beneath their feet.

Finn bent and neatly retrieved the phone the way he would snatch a fumbled football off a field of play.

"Thanks," Alvin said, wiping the moisture from his brow with his sleeve. "I lost my grip when I hit your back—which is kind of like a brick wall, by the way."

"They're called muscles, not bricks," Finn said as he resumed walking. "Next time watch where you're going and you won't need to worry."

If Finn were kind, he would say his agent's body was doughy. If he were brutally honest, he'd call Simon fat. The man spent too many hours behind a desk. The only physical activity involved walking from his office to his car. Add the fact that he never met a doughnut he didn't like, and at the age of fifty-three, he was sixty pounds overweight.

Finn tried to encourage Simon to adopt a healthier lifestyle. Unfortunately, the man was vehemently averse to change.

"Give me the claim tickets for your luggage." Alvin held out his hand then snatched it back with a sigh. "Right. You only brought a carry-on bag."

"Why didn't you stay in Chicago?" Finn asked. Alvin was a top-notch agent, capable of squeezing every penny out of a contract. But as a travel companion, he left a lot to be desired.

"You're a superstar athlete returning to play for his hometown team," Simon said, huffing to keep up with Finn's long-legged strides. "You need someone to run interference with the press."

"What press?" Finn looked around the crowded airport. When his search came up empty, he shrugged. "I asked you not to let anyone know what day I planned to arrive because I didn't want any fuss or muss. You took me at my word, right?"

"Absolutely," Alvin assured him, then muttered," Though a little pomp and circumstance wouldn't be a bad thing for your image."

"My image is just fine." Finn rolled his shoulders. "Airport photo-ops are the worst. The press conference tomorrow at the *Knights'* headquarters is soon enough for everyone in Seattle to know I'm here."

Alvin muttered something under his breath but wisely didn't enunciate enough for Finn to understand.

"All I want to do is keep my head down, remain anonymous, grab a taxi, and go home."

Home to Erin. Just the thought made Finn's weariness melt away.

"Could have at least let me arrange for a car and driver to pick us up," Alvin said. Stopping in his tracks, the agent's eyes widened. "Un, Finn?"

"What?"

"I swear." Alvin swallowed. "I had nothing to do with whatever *that* is."

Frowning, Finn followed Alvin's nervous gaze to where a small but growing crowd had gathered. At the center of attention stood a woman dressed head to toe in the Seattle Knights' official colors.

A dark blue fright wig covered the woman's natural hair while her face was painted, half gold, the other part blue. She wore a midriff-baring cheerleader's uniform with a pleated skirt that began low on her hips and ended at the top of her thighs. The hem brushed across a pair of long, shapely legs.

If her ensemble weren't eye-catching enough, she held a banner above her head. Finn's eyes widened when he read the boldly painted words.

WELCOME TO SEATTLE FINN LENNOX—FROM YOUR BIGGEST FAN

"Should I call security?" Alvin asked

To his credit, Alvin seemed willing to place his body between his client and the potentially dangerous situation. Touched, Finn moved his agent aside.

"Don't bother," Finn said, biting back a grin.

"But..." Alvin shot the woman a worried look. "She seems slightly deranged."

As if to prove the agent's point, the moment the woman spotted Finn, she waved the banner back and forth to draw his notice— unnecessary since his attention was already firmly planted on her. When her blue eyes—a color he knew well—met with his, she broke into a huge smile, dropped the banner, and made a beeline straight in his direction.

"Finny!" she shouted and performed a series of high kicks impressive enough to make a *Radio City Music Hall* Rockette turn green with envy.

"Is she out of her mind," Alvin asked, too stunned by the spectacle to do more than stare, bug-eyed.

"A little bit," Finn laughed. "But in the best way possible."

"You know her?"

Silent, Finn's grin widened just as the woman broke into a run and launched herself in his direction. Feet planted, he braced himself, catching her with skilled hands, his arms holding her tight as her legs wrapped around him like the best present ever.

"You're here," Erin whispered for his ears only as she rubbed her paint-covered cheek against his.

"And you're a freaking loon," Finn answered, not the least bit concerned.

If Erin's mental state landed her in his arms, she could take the crazy train every day of the week and twice on Sunday. Finn would happily go along for the ride.

"Now what?" Erin asked. Holding tight, she peeked at the crowd. "I spent so much time planning your welcome home, I forgot about an exit strategy."

When Erin would have slid from his embrace, Finn shook his head, holding her firmly in place.

"Relax, keep smiling, and leave everything up to me," he told her. "Alvin?"

"Uh," his agent stuttered. "Yes?"

"Taxi! Now!"

CHAPTER FOUR

DRYING HER HAIR with a towel, Erin sat on the edge of Finn's bed. Amused, she listened to his running commentary as he meticulously inspected every inch of his newly renovated closet.

The man loved his clothes, treating them with the care he might devote to a beloved child. And like any good parent, Finn didn't play favorites. His custom shoes, bespoke suits, tailored silk shirts, handstitched handkerchiefs, and soft as air underwear were all his babies.

If Finn were forced to save one item from a sinking boat, Erin sometimes feared he would simply throw up his hands at the impossible task and go down with the ship.

Yet, in many ways, Finn maintained a lighthearted approach to his wardrobe. He and Erin shared the same philosophy. What a person wore wasn't rocket science. Experiment. Take chances. Be bold. Once the fun went out of fashion, what was the point? Give everyone one choice of style in the same material and color and be done.

"Cedar lined drawers—nice," Finn said with a satisfied sigh. "How many square feet?"

"Enough to satisfy even you," she snorted. "Pace out the distance if you're curious."

When she realized Finn planned to do exactly as she suggested, Erin fell back onto the bed with a laugh.

"I had the room designed to your specifications," she called out.

"How?" Frowning, Finn stuck his head through the door. "You didn't consult with me before construction began."

Erin took a moment before she answered to admire Finn's clean-shaven face and fashionably cropped red hair. He'd rocked the beard as well as anyone, but as she told him, it was a shame to hide such a pretty face.

"Three springs ago when we vacationed in Milan, you made a drawing of your dream closet," Erin explained. "Remember?"

"Wasn't I half-drunk?" Finn asked as he continued to explore.

"You were also half-sober," she explained.

"What's the difference?"

Erin understood the distinction even if Finn didn't. Without alcohol, Finn was first and foremost, an athlete. He tended to bury his artistic side in favor of the kind of linear thinking that helped him play the game of football at the highest level.

However, when Finn drank—not too much but just enough—the left side of his brain took over from the right. On the rare occasions when he allowed his artistic side to emerge, Erin was allowed a glimpse at the person he might have been if he hadn't decided to pursue a career in professional sports.

Erin didn't believe in a life filled with what-ifs. Knocking your head against the wall over what might have been was the quickest way to a scrambled brain.

Be grateful for the gifts you have, her mother liked to say. For Erin, her greatest joy was Finn. Every day, she was grateful to have him in her life.

Some might call the pride Erin felt when she looked at him delusional. The tall, lean yet muscular body was of his own making—his and the fortunate combination of genes passed down from his parents.

When describing Finn's face, an enthusiastic sports columnist once said he had the bone structure of a god. Erin teased him mercilessly for months, but she couldn't argue with the assessment. His dark auburn hair and misty gray eyes were a gift from his

Scottish ancestors with skin that ran toward fair but tanned easily and took on a golden hue when exposed to the sun.

Physically, Finn had the perfect athlete's body, and he worked his backside off to maintain optimum performance on and off the field. He was meticulous about what he ate. A semi-vegetarian—he loved fresh fish and chicken too much to abstain—and chose organically grown whenever possible.

Erin admired Finn's self-discipline and knew that he took good care of himself for his sake as well as hers. If he stayed fit and vigilant, the chances of injury were greatly reduced.

Not that Erin didn't worry. Football was a brutal game and recent studies proved what she told Finn all those years ago when he announced his intention to try out for the high school team.

The long-term of playing football were harsher and more frightening than Erin realized.

Everyone knew that a career could end in a second. Broken bones—broken bodies—didn't always heal properly. Sometimes, no matter how hard he worked, never returned to the game he loved. Early retirement was the only option.

Finn was lucky. In all the years he'd played, after all the hits and collisions, and falls, the worst his body had suffered was a severely sprained knee. Though he balked and argued and raised holy hell to get back with his team, the doctors kept him out for two games.

If Erin had her way, Finn would have missed more time. But she learned the hard way that her influence on his life stopped once he crossed the clearly delineated lines on a football field.

For now, Finn was healthy in mind and body. Erin prayed every day that when he finally retired, he turned out to be one of the lucky ex-athletes who were blessed with long, relatively pain-free lives.

"How did you remember every little detail?" Finn asked. With a bemused expression, he joined her on the bed. "Everything in the closet is perfect."

Reaching under the bed, Erin retrieved the paper she had framed that contained Finn's elaborately detailed sketch and notes.

"I can't believe you saved it." Finn shook his head.

Knowing how fastidious Finn could be about such things, Erin carefully deposited her damp towel in the clothes hamper. Tightening the belt on her robe, she returned to the huge king-sized bed and leaned her back against the padded headboard, her shoulder brushing his.

"Even then, I hoped you'd move back to Seattle one day." Because his legs were annoyingly longer than hers, her foot only reached far enough to tap against his linen-covered calf. "If you wish hard enough, some dreams do come true."

Finn draped his arm around her. Gently, he pressed Erin's head to his chest. Smiling, she snuggled close as she enjoyed the feel of his silk shirt against her skin. Comfortable with his affectionate nature, she didn't give a second thought to how perfectly her body fit against his.

"Are wishes all you need?" With a deep rumble to his voice, he smoothed the hair from Erin's forehead. "I've held the same desire for a long time. So far, all that my efforts have delivered is a big, fat goose egg."

"You have a dream you haven't shared with me?" Erin felt equal parts surprise and hurt. Finn told her everything. Didn't he? "What do you consider a long time?"

"Seventeen years."

"You were just a kid." Feeling better, Erin shrugged. "Maybe you should give up."

"Never," Finn said. He took her hand. Slowly, he ran his thumb along the side of hers. "Some things—some people—are worth the wait."

Erin's breath caught in her chest, her heart racing. A tingling of unease skirted along her spine combined with a different, more troubling emotion she didn't care to analyze. She felt they hovered near a danger zone. One step the wrong way could be disastrous.

"Aren't you hungry?" she asked.

Keeping her tone light, Erin patted Finn's stomach and casually disentangled herself from his warm, inviting body. Wise to her plan, he kept a firm grip on her hand, stopping her before she could make a strategic retreat.

"You're the most curious person I know," he said. "Yet, you won't ask what my dream is about? *Who* it's about?"

What could she say, Erin wondered? *Don't tell me?* The trouble was, if she were perfectly honest with herself, part of her wanted to know. The other part was afraid that if Finn uttered another word, too many things would change in ways neither of them could anticipate. For the good or the bad, right now, she didn't want to find out.

"You should see the terror in your eyes." Finn sighed and brushed a finger down along the bridge of her nose. "Relax. I won't push."

Sliding from the bed, Erin felt she'd dodged a bullet. The reprieve was temporary when Finn added a caveat.

"For now."

Erin whirled around, determined to set Finn straight—about what, she wasn't sure. But he was already on his feet and headed toward the bathroom, unbuttoning his shirt as he went.

"You're right. I am hungry," he said. "I'll change and meet you downstairs in twenty minutes."

"Finn…"

"Need more time?" With a shrug, he smiled. "Half an hour. I'll drive, you pick the restaurant."

"I already made reservations." Erin tried to gather her thoughts, but Finn wasn't making the job easy. "Do we need to talk? Clear the air?"

"Pristine as a cloudless day in May on my part," Finn told her. He met her gaze. If she wasn't mistaken, she saw a flash of sympathy in his gray eyes. "When you want real clarity, let me know. I have a lot to say, but I don't think you're quite ready to listen."

Finn removed his shirt, leaving Erin with the sight of his firm, toned chest as the door closed with a light click. Erin would have preferred a jarring slam. Maybe the noise would have dispelled the image of his half-naked body from her brain.

Needing a distraction, something, anything, to fuel her ire and cool her blood, Erin latched on to the first thing that popped into her head.

"Where are my tulips," she yelled.

When Finn poked his head out the door all Erin could see was his face and a set of wide, bare shoulders. He had time to undress. Was the rest of him bare too?

Bad, Erin, she thought, silently chastising herself. Finn is your best friend. *Do not* picture him naked. Naturally, once the idea was planted in her head, she did just that. And the view was spectacular.

"Did you say something?" he asked. His expression was innocent, but his smile? Not so much.

"Flowers." Erin huffed, determined not to let her imagination—and Finn's beautiful face, get the better of her. "You always bring me red tulips. Where are they?"

Finn just smiled.

"You forgot," she accused. Erin did, too—until now. But she wasn't about to tell Finn.

"I remembered," Finn told her. When her frown deepened, his smile widened. "Did you expect me to carry a bouquet of fresh flowers on the plane from Chicago?"

"No," Erin admitted, then lifted her chin, unwilling to concede the fabricated argument. "Maybe."

"Check your office at the clinic," Finn said. "Since I didn't want to present you with limp tulips, I scheduled the delivery for first thing tomorrow morning."

"Oh." Erin felt the wind go out of her self-inflated sails. Annoyed with Finn, and herself, she sighed. "I'm hungry."

"Then move your pretty ass. You had thirty minutes." Finn looked at his watch. "Down to twenty."

Erin waited until Finn was out of sight before she stomped her feet. Childish? Yes. Necessary? Definitely.

"Why are you acting as if you've never seen a man with his shirt off," Erin chastised herself as she walked down the hall toward her bedroom. "You're almost thirty-six years old and hardly a virgin. Stop acting like one."

The sight of Finn's chest was nothing new. How many times had she seen him in nothing but a pair of swim trunks? Dozens? More. Yet for some reason today everything felt different. *She* felt different.

Erin blamed Finn.

"I've known him for almost two decades," Erin muttered as she entered her room. "Always mature beyond his years, suddenly, he decides to act like a teenager hopped up on hormones?"

Trouble was, she was no better

Erin glanced in the mirror, distressed to see a flush of red covering her cheeks. She felt her pulse. *Too fast.* Breathing deep, she concentrated on getting her emotions under control.

"Nothing has changed," she reassured herself. "Right?"

Looking at her reflection one more time, Erin didn't like what she saw. Always confident when faced with any question, for the first time in her life, she didn't have the answer.

CHAPTER FIVE

FINN HADN'T PLANNED to start his campaign to woo Erin so soon. He thought he'd take a few days. Acclimate to his new surroundings while he let her get used to having him around on a full-time basis.

Sometimes when engaged in combat—and make no mistake, Finn knew he was about to start the battle of his life—you needed to improvise. As they lay on his bed, Erin in his arms, the moment felt right. Natural.

Subtle was the best way Finn could describe the first foray. He didn't come right out and tell Erin he loved her. He used a different method—sexual attraction. He needed to know if she could see him as a man, not just a friend.

The results of Finn's impromptu experiment went better than he could have imagined.

Erin kept her head in emotionally charged situations better than anyone Finn knew. As a doctor, she always had to stay calm and even keeled. Not to say she didn't care about her patients. She did. Sometimes too much. But when the heat was on, she remained cool and never lost her head.

Lucky for Finn, he had an advantage. He knew how to push Erin's buttons. No one, not her family, not her friends, knew how to get under her skin the way he could.

Of course, Erin possessed the same skill where he was concerned. The secret was to strike first. Not always possible at the start of a genuine argument—of which they had many in their storied past.

When the attack was calculated, Finn thoroughly enjoyed watching blood boil.

Today, for the first time, he witnessed a new phenomenon. Finn saw Erin's sexual temperature rise for him. To be honest, the feeling was heady—and contagious. One of the best parts of physical intimacy with another person was the rush of feeding off her desire.

Nothing was better than wanting someone who wanted you in return. After years of subverting his desire for Erin, he was ready to let his emotions run free. Maybe, hopefully, she was ready to take the journey by his side.

As Finn parked the car on the street outside a small, neighborhood restaurant, he couldn't deny he felt a bit smug. Opening the passenger side door for Erin, he smothered the emotion. If he let himself get cocky, he could easily lose his precarious advantage.

Finn tucked Erin's hand into the crook of his arm. Her body stiffened, just for a second. A sure sign she was aware of him in a new and unsettling way. He swallowed a grin.

"I can walk from the car to the restaurant on my own," Erin told him.

Erin sounded annoyed but Finn noticed she didn't make any attempt to pull away. Unless she harbored a nefarious plan to lull him into a false sense of security—which knowing how her brain worked was always a possibility—he considered the natural brush of her body against his to be a good sign.

"I like your dress." Finn touched the capped sleeve, allowing his fingers to linger against Erin's bare skin just long enough to spike her awareness of him. "Yellow is one of my favorite colors."

"Really?" Erin asked, then shrugged as though she forgot. "I just grabbed the first thing in my closet."

Liar, Finn thought, thinking about how much time he spent picking his casual yet elegant suit from the selection of items that he sent ahead of his arrival in Seattle. He debated whether to wear a tie before choosing pale lavender to compliment the darker purple of his jacket and pants. Shoes? A pair of highly buffed, slate gray colored wingtips.

The watch on Finn's wrist sported a white face, platinum trim, and a gray leather band. Poking jauntily from his coat pocket, a silver handkerchief dotted with purple stars.

Taking time with his appearance wasn't new. But tonight, Finn took extra care. Admiring Erin's upswept hair, he knew she did the same.

The subtle sparkle of the dangling emeralds she wore in her ears. The slingback pumps the color of ripe wheat with four inches of spiked heels that brought the top of her head even with his eyes. And the slight, but unmistakable aroma of sweet lemons—his favorite scent.

Whether Erin realized it or not, tonight, she dressed for him.

As they arrived at the restaurant, Finn's phone rang.

"I meant to turn the damn thing off," he said with an apologetic frown. "My agent."

"No problem." Erin shrugged, tugging him back to the sidewalk, away from foot traffic, so they didn't block the door. "Take the call."

"Unless you're dying, I don't want to know," Finn told Alvin, his tone brusque.

"I sent you something. Watch." Alvin rushed his words as though afraid Finn might hang up if he didn't make his point as quickly as possible. He wasn't wrong. "Text me if you want to take action."

"Something wrong?" Erin asked.

"Unlikely," he said, tapping the link. After a few seconds, he grinned and handed the phone to Erin. "You're trending."

"What are you talking about?" Erin frowned.

Silently, she watched the video some resourceful traveler posted of her performance at the airport. Looking up from the screen, she met Finn's amused gaze and shrugged.

"You aren't upset?" he asked. "The thing already has ten thousand views."

"Why should I care?" she wanted to know. "I'm unrecognizable. Read the comments. Nobody has any idea who the crazy lady is."

"Someone might identify you," Finn pointed out. "What will happen to your reputation as one of Seattle's most respected and sought-after doctors if people discover what a goofball you can be?"

"Why would anyone care?" Erin dismissed the idea with a wave of her hand. "If anything, I brought myself down to earth. Made myself less godlike."

"Godlike," Finn scoffed, laughing when she winked. He should have known Erin would see the humor in the situation. "If you like, Alvin can make noise and try to get the video taken down."

"I went in knowing the chances were good someone would record us," Erin said. "No big deal. Though I resent the aspersions to my mental state. Crazy? Hardly."

As Erin straightened Finn's already perfectly aligned tie, a shadow flitted across her clear blue eyes.

"What about you?" she asked. "Will my antics cause you any trouble?"

Finn raised his arm, trapping her hand against his chest. His smile was wide and a bit wolfish.

"You read the comments. Men think you're hot, which only ups my reputation as a ladies' man. As for the women?" Finn waggled his eyebrows. "They want a man to carry *them* out of an airport. Preferably, they would prefer the man to be me."

"Great," Erin muttered. "As if your ego wasn't big enough already."

"You changed my life all those years ago," Finn said, his heart heating up as he squeezed Erin's hand. "Made me strong—in mind and body. Allowed me to believe in myself. When my Dad wanted to clip my wings, you taught me to fly."

A pleased flush of pink suffused Erin's cheeks. Strong, capable, talented, and wonderfully self-aware—most of the time—she could pass out compliments until the cows came home. But she wasn't as skilled at receiving praise as handing it out.

Did he see a trace of regret in Erin's eyes when she slid her hand from under his? Finn hoped so.

"You made all the changes," she said. "All I did was cheer you on."

"But not from the sidelines," Finn teased. "To this day, you still haven't attended a single one of my games."

"Don't blame me." Erin shrugged. "You were warned."

"I still have your promise tucked right in here. And here." Finn tapped his temple. Then, his heart. "When I play in the Super Bowl, you'll be there. Live and in person. Remember?"

"As if I could forget. You remind me annually." Lucky for me, your team never managed to make it out of the first round of the playoffs."

"Not this year," Finn told her. "The Knights are poised to repeat as champions. With me added to the mix, we're golden."

"What do you always say?" Erin asked. "In sports, there are no guarantees."

"Any given Sunday, any team can win." Finn nodded, his gaze narrowing. "You want us to lose. You want *me* to lose?"

"All I've ever wanted was for you to have everything your heart desires." Erin's lips lifted into a half-smile. "Where football is concerned, why must I watch?"

"Everything my heart desires?" Finn asked, zeroing in on the part of Erin's declaration that mattered to him the most.

"We should go in," Erin said. Deftly sidestepping his question, she rubbed her arms. "A little chilly out here. Don't you think?"

Finn had the answer he wanted, even if Erin didn't say the words. Nodding, he reached around her and opened the door to the restaurant.

"You should have brought a jacket," he admonished.

"I didn't want to crush the pleats on my dress," she countered. "Fashion before comfort. You of all people should understand."

"I'm not the one who's bare-armed in fifty-degree weather."

"But you are the one who kept me standing in the Seattle mist." Erin laughed when Finn's phone buzzed again. "Busy man."

Finn glanced at the screen. His free hand tightened into a fist. Without a second thought, he turned off the power.

"I was only teasing," Erin said. "Go ahead and answer."

"Go inside," Finn urged.

"Finn." Erin waited until they were seated to speak. "Who called."

"My dad." Finn rubbed his temple, determined the pressure he felt behind his eyes would not turn into a headache.

"No way to hide the fact that you're back in Seattle for good." A worried frown formed between Erin's brows. "Is he gambling again?"

"When did he stop?"

"I thought he finally joined a help group."

Erin knew his father's history. Jerry Lennox gambled. Not in a Hollywood movie, glamorous kind of way. He used the death of Finn's mother as an excuse to throw his life into the gutter.

To give his dad a small amount of credit, Finn doubted he wanted to pull his son down with him. To his detriment, the reasons were purely selfish. The more successful Finn became and remained, the more money Jerry could mooch to cover his debts and place new ones.

"*Gambler's Anonymous.* He went once. Or so he claimed." Frustrated, Finn slapped his hand onto the table. "Can we not talk about him? Please? Not tonight."

Nodding, Erin picked up her menu.

"Did you notice the food here is completely organic?" she asked. "I know how stringent you are about what goes into that athlete's body. Even wine was produced without pesticides or chemical fertilizers. Would you like a glass?"

Relieved, grateful that Erin didn't need or expect him to explain further, Finn took a moment to decide on his meal. Motioning for the waiter, he gave his order.

"No alcohol for me. I'm driving. You go ahead," he told Erin when she hesitated.

"I'm not really in the mood tonight," she said, settling on the shrimp scampi.

"Afraid what you might do after a few glasses of Chablis?" Finn teased. "Not to worry. The first time we kiss, I insist that you're stone-cold sober. No blaming the alcohol the morning after."

"Are you taking some kind of new supplement?" Erin demanded.

Thoroughly enjoying her discomfort, Finn sipped his water.

"Nope." Casually, he raised a questioning brow. "Why?"

"Somethings off. Maybe you should see your doctor for a blood workup," Erin said with a shake of her head. "Your sexual aggressiveness toward me is just weird."

Finn had to laugh.

"If a little flirting qualifies as sexual aggression, what kind of guys do you date lately?"

As if on cue, dressed in loose-fitting khaki pants, a sweater the color of dirty mustard, and a dark jacket desperately in need of a good pressing, a man approached the table. Average height, slender, and with a face Finn generously called handsome—if you liked the type with a week chin—the guy didn't look happy.

"I thought you canceled our date because you needed to deal with a family matter," the man said. His angry gaze flicked over Finn before landing on Erin. "Instead, I find you out with someone else? And a pretty boy to boot?"

"Pretty boy?" Finn's lips twitched as Erin released an annoyed sigh. Reluctantly, she made the introductions.

"Paul, this is Finn. Finn, Dr. Paul Kelly. We're colleagues at *Seattle General*."

Finn refused to go as far as to say he was glad to meet the man— or shake a hand that might have touched an intimate part of Erin's body. Basic manners dictated he make some sort of greeting, though he wasn't above tossing manners out the window under the right circumstances.

As though reading his mind, Erin sent him a pleading look, begging him not to make a scene. For her, he tried.

"Dr. Kelly," he said, inclining his head.

"Finn is practically my brother."

Erin's laugh grated hard on Finn's nerves.

"I'm not your brother," he told her. For emphasis, he repeated himself to Dr. Kelly. "I'm *not* her brother."

"Close enough," Erin said.

Finn shook his head. He was willing to give Erin a lot of leeway on a lot of subjects. Whether they were or weren't siblings was not one of them.

"We can do a DNA test if you like." The smile Finn gave Dr. Kelly did not reach his eyes. "Kind of a waste of time, since I'm not Erin's brother. But if you'd feel better knowing for certain, what the hell."

Dismissing Finn as not worth the effort, Paul Kelly turned to Erin, making no effort to hide the contempt in his eyes.

"You should think twice about getting involved with a younger man, Erin," he sneered. "Especially at your age."

Uh, oh, Finn thought. Dr. Kelly just entered dangerous ground. Erin didn't like someone telling her what to do, especially when every word from the man's mouth dripped with condescending superiority.

"Last time I looked, you still have twelve years on me," Erin pointed out with admirable calm. "Do you mean to say that a man heavily pushing fifty can date someone in her thirties without anyone blinking an eye? Yet I'm a dirty old woman for having dinner with a man who's barely five years my junior."

Suddenly aware that they were the center of attention, Paul tugged at the neck of his sweater as though the garment was suddenly cutting off his air supply. Sweat glistened on his upper lip.

"For months, as you pursued me from one end of the hospital to the other, you swore I didn't look a day over twenty-five," Erin said, unwilling to let her colleague off the hook just because he looked ready to hyperventilate.

"Please," Finn scoffed. "I can't believe you fell for such a lame line."

"I didn't," Erin told him. "The only reason I agreed to go out with him was that Dr. Kelly is a respected pediatrician and agreed to volunteer his time at my women's clinic."

Now Finn understood. He never cared for Erin's taste in men— mostly because he was predisposed to hate anyone she liked. But for a moment, he feared her standards had deteriorated beyond his comprehension.

"Besides, I like that I'm thirty-six," she said.

"Thirty-five," Finn corrected. "Your birthday isn't for another month."

"Close enough. I'm in my prime—sexually and physically," Erin declared. "And I plan to stay that way for many years to come. Right, Finn?"

"*Decades* to come," Finn nodded. And he planned to be right beside her as she aged with beauty and grace.

"Wait." Paul peered closely at Finn. "Are you Finn Lennox? The football player?"

"Yes."

"I'm sorry I didn't recognize you, man." Paul grinned. "I'm a big fan."

"Really?" Erin exclaimed. With a disbelieving laugh, her head fell into her hands. "First he's jealous. Then insulting. Now, he's freaking Joe Super Fan."

"You should probably move along," Finn suggested, making a shooing motion in Dr. Kelly's direction.

"Oh. Sure," Paul nodded eagerly. He paused, chewing his bottom lip. "Um, Finn?"

Suddenly they were on a first-name basis? Were they buddies? Finn rolled his eyes. *Not bloody likely.*

"Can I have your autograph?"

Finn recognized the symptoms. He'd met hundreds of people just like Erin's colleague. Dazzled to be in such close vicinity of someone whose skills on the football field he admired and maybe envied, the man appeared ready to do anything his hero suggested.

Go jump into Puget Sound came to mind.

Never one to abuse his fans—no matter how tempting the notion—Finn took the pen and paper the doctor produced from his jacket. As Erin let out a noise somewhere between a scoff of disbelief and a derisive snort, he scribbled his name.

Happy, practically beaming like a kid on Christmas morning, Dr. Kelly bowed before scampering off.

"You should have taken his number," Erin said.

"Excuse me?" Finn asked with a laugh. He couldn't wait to hear what was going on behind her clear blue eyes.

"Aren't the two of you dating now?" she asked. "Hearts practically shot from Paul's eyes. And you?"

"Yes," Finn asked.

The waiter arrived with their food before Erin could continue. Not that she was deterred. When they were alone, she picked up her mini rant right where she left off.

"You're a natural-born flirt," she said, spearing her food with more force than necessary.

"Have mercy," Finn sighed. "The poor shrimp is already dead."

Erin ignored him.

"Woman or man, you can't control yourself. And poor Paul. You batted those long eyelashes, and he was a goner. By the end, I'm sure I smelled the scent of love in bloom."

"Now I'm the villain?" Finn shook his head in wonder. "Tell me, Erin. Are you mad at me, or the fact your would-be boyfriend transferred his crush from you to me without blinking an eye?"

"He did shift loyalty with unsettling speed," Erin sighed, then laughed. "Honestly, I'm not angry with either of you. Paul can be annoying, but he's a good, compassionate doctor."

Finn nodded. Erin could forgive a person many sins if he cared about his patients.

"I found your Dr. Kelly to be a major asshat. However, if you want to let the jerk-wad off the hook, so will I."

"First, he isn't mine—heaven forbid." Smiling, Erin wiped the corner of her mouth. "Second? *You* gave him an autograph."

"Muscle memory," Finn explained. "I've signed so many of the damn things, if you put a pen anywhere in the vicinity of my hand, I automatically write my name."

"Good information to know if I ever need a loan." Erin winked. "Eat. Your food is getting cold."

They ate in the kind of comfortable silence seldom achieved unless you knew and liked your companion over a long timeframe. Finn enjoyed every bite of his grilled tuna. Out of habit and the knowledge of how easily he gained weight if he wasn't careful, he set aside his plate, a third of his meal left untouched.

Erin, on the other hand, finished every morsel and wasn't above sending him a smug smile as she licked the last drop of butter from her fork. If he didn't love her so much, Finn thought with a grin, he might hate her guts.

Nope, he decided. *Never going to happen.* Looking into Erin's laughing blue eyes, he felt a familiar catch in the region of his heart. In all the years he'd known her, he could count on one hand the times they were angry enough with each other not to speak. Once, a week went by before she broke down and called. The days between were torture.

Erin wasn't simply the love of his life. To him, she was as vital as breathing.

CHAPTER SIX

ON THE DRIVE home, sated and content from an excellent dinner and better company, an unsettling thought suddenly entered Finn's mind. Keeping his eyes on the rain-slick streets, he shot Erin a worried glance.

"How did he know where to find you?"

Erin blinked at Finn's abrupt, non sequitur question.

"Who is he?" she asked before she realized what he meant. She laughed. "You think Paul staked out my apartment then followed us to the restaurant? No, you're wrong."

Erin might think the idea was ridiculous. Finn wasn't convinced. He had a brief, but memorable stalker incident in the middle of his rookie season. The fan turned out to be harmless, but after dealing with a bodyguard, the police, and some unwanted publicity, he never forgot how one person's obsession could turn your life topsy-turvy.

"How do *you* explain Dr. Kelly's sudden appearance?"

"Coincidence," Erin said with a shrug.

"The man just happened to show up at the same small, out of the way organic-based restaurant as you? Same night. Same time?" Finn shook his head. "Highly unlikely."

"Paul was on a date," Erin told him.

"How do you know?" he asked.

"When he returned to his table, didn't you notice the cute little brunette who tried, unsuccessfully, to hide under her menu?"

Finn felt the weight of concern for Erin's safety slowly lift from his chest.

"I'll give the guy props for rebounding so quickly after you canceled on him." Noticing Erin's sour expression, Finn raised one brow. "Are you jealous?"

"Hardly," she scoffed. "However, I recognized his date. She's a nurse at *Seattle General*. She's six years my junior. Which makes her how many years younger than Paul? You do the math."

"Eighteen," Finn piped in before he realized Erin already knew the answer. "What's the real problem? I didn't think you cared about age. Yours, mine, or anyone else's."

"I don't." Erin brushed aside the idea. "What rattles my bones is the double standard. We're two decades into the twenty-first century and women still have to contend with the archaic notion that men get better with age while they just get old."

"When did you ever get the idea that life was fair?" Finn asked. "Aren't you the one who always said that the only way to get what you want is to embrace anyone who gives you a hand and barrel over the opposition? Fuck the haters."

"Sounds like me," Erin said, perking up. "Though I'm certain I never used the f-word."

"I'm certain you did. Often and with relish." Finn laughed. "You only started to clean up your language in the past few years."

"I sometimes miss cursing." Erin sighed. "Unfortunately, I have too many friends with impressionable children. I discovered quickly that when Aunt Erin speaks, little darlings tend to repeat the interesting words."

"You're a good auntie." Finn patted her hand.

"What I am is surrounded by overly fertile women," Erin told him. "Hasn't anyone heard of birth control?"

"Says the woman who makes a living off women giving birth," he snorted.

"Fair enough." Erin chuckled, softening. "I'm a woman of science. Yet I still think every baby is a miracle."

"Are you crying?" Finn asked.

"No." Erin blinked, showing him her eyes were dry. "But what if I did? Am I not allowed to get a little sentimental now and then? Sheesh. I'm a doctor, not a machine."

Erin rarely cried. Not because she didn't feel things deeply. She simply wasn't the type. On the rare occasions she did break down, her tears were happy. When she was angry, she came out swinging, ready to fight off the mad.

Pulling the car to a stop in the underground parking garage located under the building that housed Erin's apartment, Finn laughed when she opened her door and slid to her feet, beating him to the punch.

Erin wasn't opposed to Finn's gentlemanly gestures. Holding doors. Helping her from her seat. It simply didn't occur to her to wait for someone to do something she was perfectly capable of doing herself.

"Cry whenever you like," Finn assured her as they rode the elevator to the top. "Now that I'm around all the time, you have my permission to use my shoulder. Night or day."

Erin slipped from her shoes. The straps dangling from the fingers of one hand, she padded barefoot across the hardwood floor.

"During the day, you'll be busy with football or working out," she said over her shoulder as she poured water into a glass from a filtered pitcher. She downed half the contents in a few sips.

"True," Finn admitted. "Try to keep your tears limited to early morning or after six."

"Please." Erin laughed. "At night, you'll be too busy romancing the women of Seattle, one dazzled beauty at a time. I'll need to make an appointment if I want to cry on your big, strong shoulders."

Finn took Erin's glass from her hand. Ignoring her annoyed expression, he finished off the water in two gulps.

"No worries. I plan to spend my nights at home."

"You? Give up on women?" Erin snorted. She seemed to find the idea beyond her comprehension. "You aren't the type to embrace a celibate lifestyle, Finnegan."

"These days, I only want one woman." Finn placed the glass in the dishwasher before turning his full attention onto Erin. "As to whether or not I go without sex? I'll leave the decision up to you."

As the meaning of Finn's words sank in, right before his eyes, Erin's face turned a stark, panicked white. He was encouraged when seconds later, a blush of bright red traveled from her neck, over her cheeks and ears, all the way to the line of her hair.

Never one to break eye contact first, Erin's gaze skirted around the room before she forced herself to look him straight on.

"What is going on with you?" she demanded. "Ever since you arrived, you keep saying odd things. If I didn't know better, I'd think you…"

"Go on," Finn urged. "Finish your thought."

"Forget I said anything." Erin scrubbed a hand over her face. "I must be imagining things. Probably just need a good night's sleep."

"If you think anything will be different in the morning, you're mistaken," Finn told her as she headed for the stairs. "Erin!"

Shoulders stiff, Erin stopped on the third step. She waited but didn't turn.

"Never mind." Finn sighed. "Go. I'll see you in the morning."

Finn reminded himself that he lived with his desire for her since he was thirteen. For Erin, a switch from friend to lover was a new concept. He wanted to push her to accept their new normal.

Even if Erin rejected him—the possibility made Finn's heart sink like a rock—the least she could do was acknowledge his feelings instead of pretending she didn't understand what was going on. Then again, maybe she didn't.

Frustrated, Finn could only imagine what Erin was thinking. He promised himself to give her time. Now that he was here, sharing a home, sharing a life, he wanted to move at breakneck speed.

At the top of the stairs, Finn looked at Erin's bedroom door. He could wish for her to invite him in. But until she did, he needed to step back and give her time.

Finn knew from experience that he wouldn't die from wanting Erin. He survived most of his life while he waited for the time to be right. Now, with the moment at hand, he would wait a little longer.

Taking a deep breath, Finn sighed. In his heart, the chance to be with the woman he loved was worth any hardship. Even the knowledge she was so tantalizingly close, her scent still lingered on his clothes.

CHAPTER SEVEN

THE ABILITY TO sleep anywhere, anytime, had always been easy for Erin. From the time she was little, the second her head hit the pillow, she was out like a light. Occasionally—as all children did—she fussed and argued over her parent's idea of when good girls should be in bed. Once the covers were tucked tightly around her, she was off to slumberland within seconds.

In medical school, as an intern, then resident, with a busy, often unpredictable schedule, she quickly forgot the meaning of a good night's sleep. She was lucky to grab an hour here or a few minutes there.

Lying down. Sitting. Standing up. Propped against a wall. If Erin had a free minute, she spent her time sleeping. Her fellow overworked student doctors laughed and envied her what some dubbed her superpower. Others called it a gift from the Gods.

Either way, every second of rest counted when at any moment Erin might be called to care for a patient.

Years later, Erin had established a thriving practice that afforded her more stable working hours and the luxury of delegating the grunt work to a new generation of overworked, sleep-deprived residents.

The system of training doctors wasn't perfect. Some might call the method draconian—Erin certainly had when she was the one expected to run her ass off, day after day, month after month. However, she survived, thrived. Others simply dropped out.

Survival of the fittest was a harsh description of what doctors endured to achieve goals. Harsh, but accurate.

Last night, for the first time in her memory, Erin's superpower deserted her, stolen by one Finnegan Lennox.

If a gift from on high allowed her to sleep under any circumstances, there must have been an out clause—fine print that stated if the day came when Finn decided to turn his considerable sexual charm her way, she would never sleep again.

Tired, groggy from tossing and turning, Erin shuffled and swayed her way to the kitchen. After staring at the ceiling most of the night, she could barely open her heavy-lidded eyes. When she did, all she saw were wavy blurs of shapes and colors.

Going by memory, Erin managed to avoid crashing into any large objects before arriving at her destination. Out of desperation, she found the coffee—on the third try. Her entire body practically sighed with relief when she heard the first gurgle of liquid running into the pot. She almost cried at the first aroma of brewing bliss.

Erin leaned against the counter, closed her eyes, and tried to clear her mind. Like the night before and into the wee hours, she failed. An endless string of questions kept sleep at bay. Lord knew she did her best to use the time wisely But, try as she might, answers eluded her.

What was wrong with Finn? He'd always been affectionate. Shared hugs were common. Now and then, they held hands or shared a blanket while cuddled on the sofa. All innocent gestures of affection between comfortable, long-time friends.

Yesterday, out of the blue, something was different. When Finn brushed his hand against hers, she felt the heat in his eyes and a sizzle in his touch. On his bed, lying in his arms the way she had more times than she could count, the safe and comfortable haven of his embrace became much more.

Without warning, Finn became more than her friend. He felt different than the boy she remembered. Suddenly, he was a man. One who made Erin feel every inch the woman.

"Why now?" Erin muttered as she poured a cup of coffee.

"I'm tired of waiting."

Gasping in surprise, Erin came within inches of dumping an entire pot of scalding hot liquid on herself. Finn's quick thinking—and faster reflexes—saved her from a potentially serious burn.

Technically, Finn was the reason Erin almost had an accident. He also saved her from a trip to the emergency room. Because gratitude outweighed ire, just barely, she grumbled a reluctant thank you.

Finishing what she started, Finn handed Erin a freshly poured cup of coffee. Not a single drop spilled.

"When you hurt, I hurt," he said, grabbing a bottle from the refrigerator for himself. "What happened to the herbal coffee I gave you the last time I visited?"

"Not all of us are unreasonable health nuts," Erin said. She took her first sip and her taste buds rejoiced. "Caffeine is my friend."

Unlike you, Erin thought.

"I'm still your friend," Finn told her.

"On top of everything else, now you can read my mind?" Shocked and more than a little disconcerted, Erin took a step back. "Who are you?"

"Jesus, Erin," Finn snorted. "I'm not a pod person. You spoke your thoughts out loud."

"I did?" Erin frowned.

"Heard every word," he assured her. He lowered his face to her level, gray eyes bright and keen. "You look woozy. Did you sleep at all last night?"

Hoping to elude Finn's prying gaze, Erin lowered her chin.

"When have I ever had trouble sleeping?" she scoffed.

"Never," Finn said, then grinned. "Did *I* keep you up?"

"Don't be ridiculous."

"I'm right. Instead of sleeping, thoughts of me ran through your head." Finn looked way too pleased with himself. "Did you picture me naked?"

"You're five seconds away from getting a hand upside the head," Erin warned.

"Don't feel guilty," Finn said with a shrug. "You run around without anything on in my head all the time."

"Finnegan!"

Erin punched him in the arm. Unfortunately, Finn possessed muscles made of steel. He didn't feel a thing. She wasn't as lucky. Shaking her hand, she used her next best weapon. She glared. He simply smiled which sent her heart thumping. Damn him *and* his dimples.

"You're determined to hurt yourself this morning." Finn gently massaged her knuckles. "I'm sorry."

Erin snatched back her hand. Finn's touch did wonky things to her libido. The fact that she even thought of him in terms of her libido made her shiver—and not in a bad way.

"Too late for sorry, fella," Erin said, reminding herself to breathe. "I need an explanation."

"I understand." Finn sent her a sympathetic look before glancing at his watch. "Damn. Our talk will have to wait. I'm scheduled to meet a few of my new teammates at the Knights' headquarters. They agreed to show me around before we hit the gym for a workout."

Erin realized for the first time that Finn wore a muted-yellow tracksuit trimmed in gunmetal gray and a pair of jet-black running shoes. His hair was combed back from his fully rested face. Whether dressed in a meticulously tailored suit as he was last night or sporting a more casual look like now, the word handsome never quite did him justice and this morning was no exception.

"Let's have lunch," Erin was determined to hash out whatever was going on as soon as possible.

"Can't. The press conference, remember?" Finn looked genuinely sorry. "After management introduces me as the latest Knight, Levi Reynolds and Dylan Montgomery want to meet for a drink."

"Tell them you'll take a rain check," Erin insisted. "I know Levi and Dylan. They'd understand."

"I'm the new kid on the block," Finn told her with a shrug. "It would be bad form to blow off the team's starting quarterback and number one tight end. Between them, they run the offense."

"So?"

With a patient smile, Finn explained in the tone of voice he might use with a child under the age of six. Before the first word left his mouth, Erin felt her teeth start to grind against each other.

"On the football field, there's a hierarchy. We all bow to the head coach, but close behind comes the QB. Once the game begins, he's our leader, our general."

"Because a football game is a war," Erin said in a sing-song voice, mimicking something she'd heard a gazillion times.

"Blood will be spilled," Finn nodded. When Erin winced, he patted her shoulder. "Sorry. Sometimes I forget what wimp you are."

"Wimp?" Erin bristled. "Childbirth is no walk in the park. Every day, I deal in blood, and mucus, and afterbirth. Literally, I hold life and death in my hands. Compared to you and your silly game? Well, there is no comparison."

"I gladly and humbly concede to you," Finn said, holding up his hands in surrender.

"I should think so," Erin scoffed. "Sheesh."

"I did have a point to make," Finn said, quickly wiping the smile from his face when Erin crossed her arms. "My job is to catch passes. Levi needs to trust me, or he'll target someone else with the ball. Bonding over a drink, shooting some bull, is the first step. If we click off the field, chances are good we'll do the same when we suit up at game time."

Erin's already woozy head wasn't helped by sports metaphors and football whatever. She didn't want to talk about something she only tolerated because of him. Not when they had more important matters to discuss.

"You can run from the subject, Finnegan. But you can't hide," Erin warned. "Sooner than later, I *will* catch you."

"My dream come true," Finn said.

Behind the twinkle of mischief in his gray eyes, Erin spotted something else. An emotion she couldn't identify. An intensity that made her jumpy.

"I'm not joking."

"Neither am I." Finn stepped closer.

Erin groaned, angry at herself for retreating, alarmed when her back hit the refrigerator. Finn placed a hand on each side of her shoulders, effectively trapping her Their bodies never touched, but she felt his breath, minty and hot, against her face.

Erin suppressed a shudder of awareness, but Finn was too close not to notice. She expected him to gloat. Instead, she noticed his muscles of his arms tremble—ever so slightly.

Whatever emotions surged through Erin, Finn felt them, too. She wasn't sure if the knowledge comforted or terrified her.

"You might want to rethink the outfits you chose to run around in," Finn said.

Erin followed his gaze. When her chin hit her chest, she realized what he meant. Too groggy from lack of sleep to think straight, she forgot to pull on a robe before leaving her bedroom.

A tank top and matching undies, her usual nightwear, were fine when she was alone. Heck, she wouldn't have given the outfit a second thought before Finn decided to unilaterally change the dynamic of their relationship.

Now, the amount of skin Erin displayed felt unintentionally provocative. Her breasts were small but unfettered by a bra, they seemed to take on a mind of their own, jiggling with every inhale and exhale. And why did her nipples choose now to poke against the thin cotton of her shirt?

As a doctor, she understood some bodily reactions were automatic. As a woman, she wished for a bit more control. Talk about the ultimate betrayal.

"You've seen me in less," Erin said. She felt her upper hand slipping away by the second, but she wasn't about to admit the power shift. "The bikini I wore on the beach when we vacationed in Jamaica revealed more."

"I remember." Finn sighed, then smiled. "However, a little red bikini is different than what you have on this morning."

"How?" Erin demanded.

"We aren't surrounded by a beach filled with other people," Finn whispered as his irises darkened to a deep silver. "We're alone. Just the two of us. No one around to see if I slip my hand under your shirt. No prying eyes to care if my palm cups your breast."

"Finn." Erin uttered his name in one long, shuddering breath.

"I won't do either." With obvious regret, Finn backed away. "Until you make the first move, I promise to keep things between us strictly G-rated."

"Finnegan!"

"Okay. PG." With a crooked smile, Finn shrugged. "Maybe, PG-13 if I drop a curse word here or there."

Unable to move, unsure what just happened, Erin watched as Finn crossed to the front door. Slinging a black leather duffle bag over his shoulder, he sent her a hooded look.

"No will always mean no," he said. "If you don't want me, say the word. I'll respect your decision. However, if the answer is yes, tell me. Soon. I've waited for a long time. I can't wait much longer."

Alone, Erin slowly sank to the floor. She touched her palm to her cheeks, amazed her face could be so hot when her hand was ice cold. Closing her eyes, she remembered Finn's words.

I've waited for a long time.

Well, too bad. He blithely shoved Erin into unknown territory, then expected her to change twenty-years of thinking overnight? Not going to happen. Not in a blink of his silvery eyes. Friends to lovers was a great concept in the movies or between the covers of a book. In real life, not so much.

Erin didn't know what she wanted. But one thing was certain. Finn left the decision up to her and she would not be rushed. If he wanted fast, he could call up one of his football groupies. If he wanted her? He would just have to wait. Maybe, forever.

CHAPTER EIGHT

"WELCOME TO THE *Knights*."

Levi Reynolds lifted a glass of beer, clinking his glass against Finn's. One seat over, Dylan Montgomery joined in before taking a drink of club soda.

"Dylan's a lightweight where alcohol is concerned," Levi explained when they placed their orders. The *Seattle Knights'* starting dark-haired quarterback laughed. "All he needs to do is smell the fumes and he's under the table."

"Not quite," Dylan Montgomery shrugged. "But I agree with Levi on one thing. Welcome back to Seattle, Finn."

"Thanks. Someone once told me never to have more than one drink when I go to a bar or club." Finn pictured Erin. At the time, she was in full lecture mode. "If I had to overindulge, only do it when I'm at home."

"Good advice for anyone," Levi nodded. "Holds true especially for a public figure. The second you do anything stupid, even money says someone will post your idiocy online. Damn cell phones make everyone a reporter."

"Speaking of cell phone cameras." Dylan's blue eyes sparkled with interest. "The video of you and your *biggest fan* made quite a splash. According to Eve, the post has almost two million views since yesterday, and counting."

Finn ran a hand over his mouth to mask his grin. More than a few of those views came from him. He couldn't stay away to the point where he bookmarked the link on his phone *and* laptop. Not sure how Erin would feel if he outed her—even among friends—he cleared his throat.

"Eve? Anyone I know?" he asked, hoping to change the subject.

"Dylan's girlfriend," Levi volunteered. "You'll meet her soon along with my wife, Piper, and the rest of the team's significant others."

"Eve isn't my girlfriend," Dylan sighed.

"What the hell?" Levi slammed his glass onto the table sending a backsplash of beer over his hand. Absently, he accepted a napkin from Finn. "You barely made up—after more drama than a freaking soap opera. If Eve wised up and dumped your sorry ass for good don't come crying to me. Not this time."

"On the field, the man's cool as a blizzard in January. In real life, he's a fucking crybaby," Dylan said to Finn with a mournful expression. Reaching over, he patted Levi's arm. "Calm down. The reason Eve isn't my girlfriend is that as of this morning, she's now my fiancée."

"Congratulations." Grinning, Finn shook Dylan's hand.

"Thank God," Levi laughed. "I was afraid if she left you for good, you'd stop eating and I'd be stuck with the dog."

"Confused?" Dylan asked Finn.

"A little. But I'll figure things out," he promised. "Been a while since I joined a new team. Makes me feel like a rookie again."

"Long story short. Nana, the dog, belongs to my niece. I have custody, temporarily," Dylan explained.

"Now, about the airport video." Levi rubbed his hands together. "Who was the woman?"

Finn groaned. So much for causing a distraction.

"Must have been Erin." Levi looked at Dylan. "Right?"

"Dr. Ashmore? No way." Dylan shook his head, a strand of blond hair falling across his forehead. "She's too refined."

Caught off-guard by Dylan's observation, Finn barely managed not to spew beer across the table and onto his teammates.

"Erin might appear cool and proper on the surface," Levi said. "Once you get to know her better, you'll realize that she has a wicked sense of humor. Painting her face and dressing up like a cheerleader is exactly the kind of stunt she might pull. Right, Finn?"

Where Erin's personality was concerned, Dylan hit the nail on the head. However, if Finn agreed, he might as well admit the truth. He saw no way to quell the men's curiosity. Damned if he did, damned if didn't.

"No comment," he said.

"Good enough for me," Dylan laughed. "The cheerleader has to be Erin."

"Okay." Finn shook his head. "Can we turn to a subject less likely to put my ass in a sling?"

"Should we talk about the suit you chose to wear for today's press conference?" Levi asked with a chuckle, looking Finn up and down. "I know some football players are known for their flashy clothes, but I can't remember the last time I saw a grown man dressed head to toe in pink.

"One thing's for certain," Dylan chimed in. "You were easy to spot under the bright lights. The glare from that suit was so bad, I had to put on a pair of sunglasses before my corneas caught fire."

Finn's sense of style was all his own. Unique. Colorful. Fashion-forward. Confident in his choices, he wasn't offended by his new teammate's ribbing. Instead, he was relieved. If Levi and Dylan felt comfortable enough to give him hell, it meant they accepted him as one of their own.

"Philistines," Finn scoffed. "Let me educate you in the way of haute couture."

"Please, do," Levi snorted derisively. "Nothing we'd like better."

"Good. Listen and learn," Finn said, ignoring the QB's sarcastic tone. "The color of the suit and tie, *Armani*, by the way, is fuchsia. The hue of the shirt, silk, is called aubergine. But the socks?"

"Not the socks," Dylan pleaded. "Have mercy."

"The socks," Finn continued, lifting his pant leg and rotating his ankle *They* are what you call pink."

"Well, fuck me." Laughing, Levi slapped Finn on the shoulder. "Only a man with balls of steel would have the nerve to wear pink socks in a sports bar."

"If someone objects, you guys have my back. Right?" Finn asked, putting their fledgling friendship to the test.

"We'll definitely stand behind you when the fists start flying," Dylan nodded.

"I planned to congratulate you on the Super Bowl win. Now, I'm not so sure." Giving in, Finn laughed. This time, he was the first to raise his glass.

"Feels damn good," Levi admitted.

"Amen, brother," Dylan nodded.

Anyone who played professional football and claimed they didn't care about winning a championship, was a flat-out liar. Lifting the Lombardi Trophy in victory was the stuff little boy's— and more than a few girl's—dreams were made of. By the time they reached high school, most knew they would never reach their goal.

But for those lucky few who were good enough to make it to the NFL, the dream never died.

"What do you say I help you do it again?" Finn asked.

"Maybe." Levi held up a hand before Finn could protest. "Don't get me wrong. We plan to play every game with our blood, sweat, and tears if necessary. Down to the last second. But..."

Dylan picked up where Levi left off.

"We weren't supposed to win last year. The odds weren't even slim. They were subzero" he said. "We'll get a little more love next season. But getting back to the big game is hard enough. Repeating as champions? Rarely done. Almost never."

"I didn't come to Seattle to lose," Finn told them. "I pull my weight. Hell, if you want to jump on, I'll pull yours as well."

"Cocky bastard," Levi snorted.

"Always have been. Until now, I didn't have the talent around me to win." Sitting back, Finn looked from one man to the other, letting them see the determination in his eyes. "What do you say? Are you with me?"

On cue, Queen's *We Are the Champions* blasted from the jukebox. Laughing, Dylan almost fell off his chair.

"Sounds like an omen to me," he said once he recovered. "Levi? You're the starting QB. Are you in?"

"What the hell." Levi bumped fists with Finn. "Let's bring home another championship."

CHAPTER NINE

CIRCUMSTANCES BEYOND ANYONE'S control prevented Erin and Finn from clearing the air.

First, Erin experienced a boom in business. At her clinic and *Seattle General*, expectant mothers went into labor right and left. Some babies were right on schedule, others seemed extra eager to make their way into the world.

Second, Finn found himself inundated with requests for interviews and personal appearances. His status as a superstar player and the fact he was born and raised in Seattle added to the excitement and interest.

Didn't hurt that Finn's handsome face and lean body were a publicity agent's dream come true.

The addition of Finn Lennox to the Knights' made people who until now didn't give a flying leap about football sit up and take notice. Because Finn wanted to help the team, he was reluctant to refuse the myriad of requests for his time.

As a result, Erin and Finn barely managed to text each other, let alone meet in person. To be honest, Erin wasn't sure if she was relieved or disappointed by the unavoidable delay.

During the next eight days, rather than bother to head home only to be called back again, she decided to sleep on a make-shift bed in her office. She lived in one set of sapphire-blue scrubs after another. The color was great, her personal choice when she set up her practice. But fashion-wise, she wasn't about to make anyone's best-dressed list.

Kicking off her shoes, Erin put her feet up on her desk. She bit into a makeshift sandwich, sighing with pleasure. At this point, even canned tuna fish tasted like a gourmet delight.

"I miss my pretty bra and panty sets," Erin groused to Eileen Wymore as they took a much-needed breather between births. She tugged at the neck of her baggy shirt and let out a resigned sigh. "No point in wearing anything but plain black cotton."

"True," Erin's head nurse laughed. "Anything else would get stained with blood and sweat."

"Ah, the glamorous life of a medical professional. Thank goodness little girls who dream of being a doctor have no idea what's involved or they'd all grow up to be anything else." Erin rolled her head in a slow circle, wincing when her neck popped.

"Says the woman who loves her job—even the long hours."

"True," Erin nodded, then yawned. "Did you check on Shelly Lowenstein?"

"Her false labor turned into the real thing about thirty minutes ago." Eileen let out a tired laugh. "She wasn't due for another two weeks."

"Must be something in the air. The weather turned hot and so did our birthrate. Thank the heavens no one's experienced any complications. Smooth sailing." Erin poked a straw into a juice box and took a sip. When the flavor of orange hit the proper tastebuds, she made a happy humming sound. "Sometimes the simple pleasures are the best."

"Like eight solid hours of sleep," Eileen said.

"Try taking a nap," Erin suggested. "Even five minutes can do wonders."

"Not all of us can zonk out at a moment's notice." Eileen rubbed her tired eyes. "Every time I try, all I do is toss and turn."

"Hang on a little longer," Erin said with a sympathetic smile. "Myrna Allen's shift starts in an hour. Then, you're free for the next four days."

"Who will relieve you?" Eileen asked. "No one. I understand that your patients trust only you to deliver their babies, but you haven't had a real break in days."

"Which is why I get the big bucks."

"And the pretty flowers." Eileen sighed, nodding toward the crystal vase on Erin's desk. "As a girl, I daydreamed that a man would someday send me roses. But I have to say, red tulips aren't bad."

Erin vividly remembered when Finn gave her the first bouquet. A high school gymnasium wasn't the most romantic setting. However, back then she didn't want or expect romance. Not from him. Not from anyone. At eighteen, her eyes were filled with drive and ambition, not starry nights and glittery hearts.

Years later, Erin hadn't achieved all her goals, and a desire to succeed still burned in her gut. Tempered a bit by experience, the flame was bright and steady.

Lately, Erin wondered if she should carve out a part of her life for someone special. Problem was, none of the men she met stirred her interest in a permanent relationship. Finn was the only one she cared about but he was her friend—like family. Until he decided to stir the pot.

Erin knew she and Finn couldn't go back. He wanted more and she wanted... If she only knew.

"Must be nice to have someone to go home to," Eileen said. "I know how much you prize your privacy. But a man like Finn is the kind of company any woman would enjoy."

"We get along," Erin said. "Always have."

"He's so pretty." Laughing, Eileen fanned herself. "Even my husband has a crush."

"Finn's always been like a brother to me."

At least that's what she told herself. Lately, Erin wasn't so sure. Finn certainly made his position clear to her and anyone who wanted to listen. They weren't siblings. Period. Full stop. Now, she had to decide if she agreed.

"Dr. Ashmore?" One of the hospital's scrub nurses stuck her head into Erin's office. "You're needed in operating room four. Mother waited most of the day before she told her family she was in labor. She's almost fully dilated. Looks like a breech birth."

"Be right there." Erin tossed her half-eaten sandwich into the trash and jumped to her feet. She patted Eileen on the shoulder and sighed. "So much for smooth sailing."

FINN SPRINTED TOWARD the endzone the way he had a million times before. A defensive end was glued to his side, intent on making a name for himself on the first day of training camp by keeping the ball out of a veteran player's hands.

Good luck, kid, Finn thought. You may be a first-round draft pick, but it's time you found out that college is nothing like the NFL.

Feinting right, Finn paused long enough to throw off the rookie's timing. Then, slick as newly fallen snow, he found open ground and caught the perfectly thrown spiral right in his breadbox.

"Touchdown," Levi yelled, lifting his arms straight into the air. Jogging across the field, he stopped to pat the dejected rookie on the back. "One day doesn't make or break a career."

"You're fast," the kid said to Finn. "Faster than anyone I covered at UCLA"

"The game slows down after a while," Finn said, then laughed. "As do running backs."

"Not you," the kid said, a little dazzled by the setting and veteran players around him.

"Not yet," Finn corrected. "I still have a few years left in my legs."

"You were good with him," Levi said when the kid was out of earshot. "You knocked a little stuffing out of him with that touchdown move, then built him back up with a few kind words."

"I may be old in his eyes, but I can remember my first day." Finn watched as the kid huddled with his fellow rookies and sighed. "Though I'm not sure I was ever that young."

"Can't say I'd want to go back," Levi said. "The best time of my life is right now."

Thinking of Erin, Finn had to agree. He treasured every moment with her, past and present. If only they could find some time together so he could plead his case. Setting a romantic mood wasn't an easy thing to accomplish when he and the woman he loved couldn't find the time to be in the same room, let alone the same bed.

"Do you have any questions?" Levi asked, breaking into Finn's thoughts.

"Questions?" he frowned, wondering if the QB could read his mind.

"About our playbook." Levi laughed. "What did you think I meant?"

"Women." Finn saw no reason to lie. "Rather, one woman in particular."

"Afraid you're on your own," Levi told him.

"You're a married man," Finn said. "You must have done something right."

"Mostly, I didn't screw things up," Levi admitted. "Well, I did, as my wife will attest. Lucky for me, Piper loves me enough to overlook my mistakes."

"You can't force someone to love you," Finn muttered.

"No," Levi agreed. "But you can do your level best to move the arrow in your direction. Have you told her how you feel?"

"Not in so many words," Finn said. "She knows I want her."

"Sex." Levi nodded. "Not a bad place to start, but the worst place to finish if your heart is involved. She needs to know that you want more than just her body."

"Starting to rain." Levi held out his hand, catching the first drops as they fell from the overcast sky. "Perfect timing since practice is over for the day. Want to grab a beer?"

"Another time," Finn said.

"A prior engagement with a certain woman?" Levi asked.

When Finn shrugged, the QB smiled, nodded, and made his way to the locker room.

After a quick shower, Finn dressed in his street clothes before checking his phone. He found a message from his agent, another from his management company, and almost a dozen from his father which he deleted without reading. But nothing from Erin.

"Another night alone?" Finn asked himself as he drove from the parking lot.

Maybe Erin was too tired to text. Perhaps she was done with work and they could spend the evening together. A sudden cloudburst hit the car and Finn flipped on the windshield wipers before stopping at a red light.

Finn was lonely. He had the names of a dozen women he could call, but he only wanted Erin.

Pulling into the parking garage, Finn dreaded another night alone in the empty apartment. He knew Erin's work was important and he was proud of her success. But he missed her.

As Finn entered the elevator, he crossed his fingers. Hopefully, he had someone waiting at home.

CHAPTER TEN

THE APARTMENT WAS dark, cold, and unwelcoming. The only bit of brightness came from the bank of windows in the living room. Erin rarely closed the curtains, preferring to let in the natural light.

Tonight, the moon and stars were covered by rain-heavy clouds. Even the city lights were muted by the sheets of water falling from the sky.

Briefly, Finn considered catching a movie by himself rather than wander the apartment like a lost lamb. Pathetic, yes. With no one to witness his hunched shoulders and sad face, he gladly gave into a bout of self-pity.

With a sigh, Finn opened the refrigerator and stared at the contents. He felt a burst of warmth when he realized everything from the organic vegetables to the wheatgerm and bottled alfalfa juice were for him.

Finn knew that Erin had a stockpile of empty-calorie treats hidden somewhere. But knowing how hard he worked to maintain a healthy lifestyle, she didn't flaunt her favorite *Snickers* bars and *Ding Dongs*.

Taking a bag of raw almonds from the door, he grabbed a bottle of water and headed up the stairs without turning on the lights. As he walked into his bedroom, he glanced to his right, stopping when he noticed a pair of red and pink striped stiletto pumps strewn on the floor.

Certain the shoes weren't there when he left that morning, he walked across the hall. As Finn stooped to retrieve the pumps, his face was hit by a cool, damp burst of air.

"No reason for the rooftop door to be open," he muttered to himself. "Unless…"

Erin. Like a burst of energy to his flagging spirits, the thought she might be within touching distance sent Finn rushing up the stairs.

The rain fell hard, leaving puddles every few feet. Finn expected to find her under the canvas awning at the entrance to the garden, but Erin was nowhere to be seen.

Finn almost turned to leave before he noticed that several of the motion-sensitive lights lining the rooftop were lit—a sure sign that someone must have recently passed by.

"Erin?" he called out. "Where are you?"

"Over here."

Where was here? Finn abandoned any idea of staying dry and stepped into the rain.

Covering most of the roof, the garden was large and lush with a variety of flowers, shrubs, and greenery. Finn questioned why a woman who didn't cook—who rarely ate at home—needed more than a dozen heirloom tomato plants. But Erin saw nothing odd. She enjoyed watching the wonder of nature as the row of seedlings grew into fruit-bearing plants. Once they reached their maturity, she gave the bounty to friends and family.

Wiping the constant stream of water from his face, Finn followed the winding path that led to a raised platform at the edge of the garden. White limestone rocks crunched beneath his feet, the sound harmonizing with the splatter of raindrops as they pounded the surface of a round glass table.

"Here."

Erin's voice was faint, but this time, Finn had no problem locating the sound. She was surrounded by rose bushes. Soaked through to the skin, she stood with her back to him as she looked out at the city.

Removing his jacket, Finn covered her head, draping the material around her shoulders. Futile considering, but the gesture was instinctual. His woman was wet and shivering—end of the story. Logic could wait for another time and place.

"What are you doing?" Finn demanded.

Erin merely shrugged. Shaking his head, Finn wrapped his arms around her from behind, hoping the heat from his body would seep into hers.

"How long have you been here?"

"Can't say for certain," Erin whispered. Her head fell onto his shoulder. "Five minutes? An hour?"

"Did something happen at the hospital?" Finn wanted to know if Erin lost a patient. Because he knew how deeply she cared about everyone under her care, he left the question unasked.

"Alice Arnold had a baby."

The tears in Erin's voice were unmistakable. Finn relaxed because, for her, tears meant happiness, not sorrow.

"You delivered a lot of babies in the last week or so," he said as the deluge around them became a sprinkle. "What makes Alice Arnold's case special?"

"Alice is twenty-six. Married for less than a year." Erin sniffled. Laughed.

Finn shook his head. Funny how as the rain slowed, Erin's tears fell harder.

"A lot of young women give birth—married or otherwise," Finn said, smiling when Erin's laugh was followed by a soggy hiccup.

"When Alice was nineteen, she was diagnosed with cancer. I found the lump in her breast during a routine exam."

"Nineteen?" Finn couldn't imagine.

"Alice was adopted so she didn't know her family history. The oncologist ran some tests and discovered she carried a gene that made the chance of recurrence highly likely." Erin took a shaky breath. "Lord she was brave. Terrified—who wouldn't be—but unbelievably strong. She talked to her family, received counseling. Then, as a freshman in college, she chose to have a preventative double mastectomy."

Finn's stomach clenched. Life could be fucking unfair.

"During her senior year, Alice met her future husband." Erin wiped her cheeks. "She was afraid to tell him about her medical history. Reconstructive surgery meant her breasts looked normal, but because of the radiation and chemotherapy she went through, the possibility existed that she wouldn't be able to conceive."

If Erin went through the same thing, Finn would get down on his knees in thanks that she was alive. Nothing else would matter.

"The guy stuck by her side?"

"Without a second thought." Erin sighed. "They planned to adopt and were on several waiting lists. Then, they received their miracle. Alice found out she was pregnant."

"You told her?" Finn asked.

"Yes." Erin squeezed Finn's hand. "As a doctor, I can't remember a happier moment. Until today."

"I'm glad for Alice. And her husband," Finn said. "But why did you decide the best way to celebrate was to stand in a freaking downpour? Popping a bottle of champagne makes more sense. And is less likely to cause pneumonia."

"Healthy people don't get sick from a little rain."

"You and I have different ideas about what constitutes a *little* rain." Taking Erin by the arms, he turned her around until they faced each other. "Let's go inside. Take a hot shower while I fix some tea."

"In a minute." Erin smoothed the hair from Finn's forehead. As she brushed her thumb over his cheek, she looked into his eyes. "Finn?"

Amazed by the way the blue of her irises deepened in color, Finn allowed himself a moment to savor Erin's sweet touch.

"What do you need?" he asked. "Tell me. Anything."

"Let's have a baby."

CHAPTER ELEVEN

LET'S HAVE A baby.

Certain Erin had to be joking, Finn waited for her to laugh. Instead, she looked at him with genuine anticipation. Did she honestly expect him to say yes to such a life-changing request?

"You aren't serious." Taking her shoulders in his hands, he gave Erin a gentle shake. "I understand how the moment of helping someone like Alice bring a new life into the word might discombobulate your brain."

"My thinking is clear and focused." Erin's smile was bright as she wrapped her arms around him. "Genetically, you're practically obligated to reproduce."

"Wow. Unbelievable." Finn shook his head. "At first, I was thrown off balance and didn't know what to say. Now, I'm offended."

"Why?" Erin seemed genuinely confused.

"I told you how I feel," Finn said. "I gave you time to decide if you wanted me the same way I want you. But instead of telling me what's in your heart, you come at me with a request for my superior DNA?"

"Take a breath," she told him. "Don't let your emotions get in the way of common sense."

"What's logical about any of this?" Finn wanted to know.

"Simple," in a calm, teacherlike voice that set his teeth on edge. "Thirty-six isn't old by most standards. But if I want a baby, time is not on my side. As for you, technically, you can father a child at any age. But things like sperm count and potency begin to dwindle once you turn thirty."

All through Erin's speech, Finn wasn't sure how he felt. Now he knew. Now, he was royally and thoroughly pissed off.

"Fine. You want my DNA. Let's make a baby." Finn swept Erin into his arms. He pushed his way into the house. His jacket hit the floor, falling from her shoulders at the same time his feet pounded down the stairs. "Dwindling potency, my ass."

"Wait. Let me down."

Erin pushed at Finn's arms but soon found her efforts to be a losing battle. He didn't let go until he entered his room, kicked shut the door, then dumped her onto the bed.

Finn pulled his shirt over his head. With one flick, he unsnapped his pants. A second later he stood in front of her wearing nothing but a pair of boxer/briefs and a scowl.

"I wanted to take things slowly. Date. Hold hands. Kiss. When you were ready, then we'd make love. Emphasis on love." His temper rising with each word, Finn ran his hands through his hair. Water flew in every direction. "But if you want down and dirty, baby-making sex, no problem."

"Stop right where you are, Finnegan," Erin warned when he crawled onto the bed like a hungry lion stalking his prey.

"Call me by my full name all you want," he warned. "Won't work this time."

Erin scooted up the bed until her back hit the headboard. She was concerned more than panicked which didn't do anything to cool Finn's ire. He wouldn't force himself on her—just the idea was too abhorrent to contemplate.

However, Finn needed her to realize he wasn't an object she could use at her convenience. He was a flesh and blood man. If they ever made a baby, he wanted their child to be conceived in love, not on a whim.

"We both know you'd never hurt me," Erin said as she placed a hand on his chest in a feeble attempt to stop his forward momentum.

"I won't give you pain," Finn growled. "Only pleasure."

"I want to laugh right now so much," she snorted. "You'll only give me pleasure?"

"Do you doubt that I can make you want me?" Finn's gaze dropped to Erin's lips as he ran a hand along the inside of Erin's leg. When she let out a surprised gasp, he smiled. "Protest all you want. Your body tells a different story."

"I don't want you, Finn," Erin said in a rush. "I need your sperm. In a lab. To make a baby."

Talk about an erection killer. The woman Finn loved for most of his life just admitted she wanted his baby but without any of the fun part. With a sigh of defeat, he rolled from the bed.

"You're a real piece of work." Finn grabbed a robe from his closet. "Are you the same woman I've known for twenty years? Did you suddenly change? Or have I been blind all this time to the real you?"

"Don't be ridiculous." Erin reached for him but pulled back her hand when his gaze narrowed to a warning slit. "I thought a lot about what you said. And I believe we'd be good together."

"Then what's the problem?" Finn sat on the bed, his expression earnest. "I want children. I want them with you. If you'd like to get pregnant in six months, or a year, great."

"Friends who become lovers then break up, never go back to when they were just friends." Erin took Finn's hand in hers. "You are the most important person in my life. I can't afford to lose you."

"If we had a child, do you think we'd always be together?" Finn couldn't wrap his head around Erin's skewed form of logic. "What if I get traded to another team."

"Why would you?" Erin asked, obviously baffled. "Don't you have a no-trade clause in your contract?"

"Yes," Finn admitted. "But if the Knights wanted me gone, they could pressure me into giving my consent."

"How?" Erin frowned. "Threaten to break your legs?"

"Jesus," Finn snorted. "They're a football team, not the mafia. Instead of violence, the Knights could simply sit me on the bench. If I wanted to play, I would need to go someplace else."

"Crazy," Erin huffed. "But okay. Let's say you end up in a different city. We lived apart before."

"Damn it, Erin. Your skin is like ice." Finn pulled a thick robe from a hanger in his closet along with a pair of thermal socks and a long-sleeved cotton shirt. "Change before finish our discussion."

"Keep talking." Erin left the closet door ajar. "I can hear you."

"Yes, we lived apart for a long time," Finn agreed. "The difference would be our hypothetical baby. I want to be a part of my child's life."

Erin reentered the bedroom. Finn's robe hit her around mid-calf, and she'd rolled the too-long sleeves up to her elbows. Like the robe, his socks were too large, but with the excess material bunched at the ankles, they did the job. Sitting cross-legged on the bed, she dried her hair with a towel from his bathroom.

"You can visit us," she said. "Often."

"What if I want primary custody."

Finn could tell by the way Erin's chin hit her chest that she wasn't prepared for the wrinkle he added to her plan.

"Your job takes you on the road, mine doesn't," she argued.

"We're both busy," Finn countered. "However, when the season ends, I can spend all day with our child. Other than a few weeks of vacation, you're on the clock more often than not."

Out of arguments, Erin frowned. Before she could reload, Finn decided the best thing was to get a good night's sleep and start again in the morning. He wasn't ready to give her what she wanted. Neither was he ready to abandon his dream of living the rest of his life beside the woman he loved.

"Let's talk again in the morning." Finn tugged Erin from the bed and pushed her toward the door. "I need time to think. You do the same."

In the hallway, Erin turned to Finn. Meeting his gaze, she absently played with the tie to his robe.

"You think I haven't given my proposition enough thought. Maybe you're right." She shrugged. "The more I think about a little Finn, red hair and gray eyes, running around, the more I like the idea."

"I would love a little blonde-haired, blue-eyed, Erin." Finn smiled at the image. "But I want a child the old-fashioned way. If we can't conceive, there are a lot of kids out there who need a home."

"Seems we do have a lot to think about," Erin nodded, then sighed. "I know one thing for certain.

"What's that?" Finn asked.

"My life would be very sad without you."

"Then be happy." He placed a kiss on her forehead. "I'm not going anywhere."

"Promise?"

Finn opened his arms. His heart soared when Erin walked into his embrace.

"I will fight anyone who tries to take me away—human, demon, or deity."

"Finny," Erin laughed. "You know how I feel, right? Always."

Love. Erin's definition might be different than his, but the emotion was just as real. Just as firmly ingrained. Just as permanent.

"I know," Finn nodded, pulling her tight. "I feel the same. Always."

CHAPTER TWELVE

ERIN DIDN'T ENJOY eating breakfast. No matter how hard she tried to muster a semblance of enthusiasm, her appetite didn't officially kick into gear until lunchtime. If she rolled out of bed several hours early or worked out before sunrise—yuk—to fool her metabolism, it didn't matter.

Food simply did not appeal to her before noon.

Where breakfast was concerned, Finn was Erin's complete opposite. He not only enjoyed a hearty meal at the crack of dawn whenever they were together, but he also harped and cajoled and nagged until she gave in and gagged her way through half of a bowl of cereal just to shut him up.

"You haven't had anything to eat for close to twelve hours," he would tell her. "Your body needs fuel. Do you want to faint from hunger while in the middle of doing your rounds?"

"No big deal," Erin shot back. "If I have to collapse, can you think of a better place than at a hospital?"

The history of their arguments over her eating habits was long and varied. Nothing ever changed—at least not where Finn was concerned. As Erin discovered the next morning.

As Erin descended the stairs, her stomach was in knots at the thought of facing him after their baby discussion of the night before, she wiped her damp hands on her pale-yellow linen pants. She found Finn in the kitchen. Humming along with the latest from Bruno Mars, he expertly slid an egg white omelet onto a plate before pouring something the color of green slime from the blender into two waiting glasses.

"Must you be so disgustingly chipper at such an ungodly hour?" Erin asked. Taking Finn's phone off the counter, she stopped the music. "Ah. Quiet. That's how the morning should sound."

"As always, you're a burst of sunshine to start the day." Finn laughed when Erin stuck out her tongue. He handed her a glass of goo. "Sit. Drink."

Erin sniffed the vile concoction. The odor reminded her of dirt, with an overlay of moldy grass.

"Why do healthy things always smell like week-old garbage?" she wanted to know as she slid the drink across the counter.

"If you want to get pregnant, you need to fill your body with the proper nutrients."

"I'll take a daily supplement," she muttered. Then, realizing what Finn said, her eyes widened. "Did you say pregnant? You decided we should have a baby? Really?"

Finn placed his hands on her shoulders as if afraid she might float away in her excitement.

"Calm down," he told her, a half-smile curving one side of his mouth. "And don't get ahead of yourself. I did a lot of thinking last night."

"You look fully rested," Erin scoffed. Hair damp from his shower, dressed in a bright purple designer t-shirt—his one concession to fashion—and a pair of well-worn blue jeans, he was gorgeous—nothing new. And sexy. Okay, *that* was new. At least in her eyes.

"I think while I sleep."

Finn guided her to one of the stools that lined one side of the silver-flecked granite countertop. Once she was seated, he sat the weird smoothy she'd already rejected in front of her.

"One sip," he told her.

"If I vomit, you get to clean up the mess," Erin warned.

"Deal," Finn nodded.

Tentatively, her face scrunched up in dreaded anticipation, Erin dribbled a teaspoon-sized amount of the viscous liquid past her lips, gagged, then swallowed.

"Ugh." Erin covered her mouth in case her stomach rebelled. "Feels like snot rolling down my throat."

"Your descriptive powers are as impressive as always," Finn sighed. Shaking his head, he downed the contents of his glass in five long gulps.

"Good for you," Erin said with a shudder. 'You'll live to be a hundred. As will I. But without a steady diet of whatever you call that slop."

"Promise?" Finn asked as he dumped Erin's drink down the garbage disposal.

"What should I promise you?" she asked with a confused frown.

"If you don't live to be a hundred? If you die and leave me alone? I'll never forgive you."

The teasing light was gone from Finn's eyes. Erin tried not to smile. He might have the body of a grown man, but for an instant, she caught a glimpse of the scared, vulnerable ten-year-old boy whose desperate need for a friend broke her heart all those years ago.

"If I have my way," she said. "We'll be together until our bones turn to dust."

"If you drank more milk, you wouldn't need to worry about your bones," he told her with a wink.

And just like that, lighthearted Finn was back. Erin laughed, accepting the apple he peeled and quartered. Compared to the slimy smoothy, she chewed and swallowed the fruit with ease.

"You think you're clever," Erin said as she bit into the second piece. "You always planned for me to eat something. The slime was just a decoy."

Finn leaned a jean-covered hip against the side of the counter. He took a bite of omelet and shrugged.

"I've learned a trick or two from you over the years," he said. "Including how to handle a picky eater."

"I'll eat almost anything," Erin protested. "But *not* in the morning."

"And yet, you finished the whole apple." Finn shot her a smug smile. "Admit it. I'm good."

"You'd be good with our little boy or girl," Erin said. "Children can be notoriously picky eaters."

"Smooth segue." Finn chuckled. He placed his plate in the dishwasher before facing her again, arms crossed. "I have a counter-proposal."

"I don't want to get married just to have a baby," Erin told him in a rush.

"Not *that* kind of proposal, knucklehead." Finn cleared his throat. "Give me until the end of the football season."

"To do what?" she asked.

"You never let me finish," Finn said with a frustrated sigh.

"Because you always take the long way around every subject," Erin told him. "I always tell you to be concise and to the point. But do you learn? Nope. Instead, you use ten words when one would do. How we became friends, I'll never know."

"Now who's rambling," Finn asked with a snort.

"Fair point," Erin agreed. "Please continue."

"First let me clear up a point you raised," Finn said. "We became friends because you're a pushy know-it-all. A fact for which I am eternally grateful."

"I take exception to the term know-it-all." Erin laughed because his description of her wasn't far off. "What's your second point?"

"I propose we date each other for the duration of the football season." Holding her gaze, Finn tipped his head a little to the side. "Twenty-three weeks, including the pre-season and a bye week."

Erin frowned. Almost six months. The math wasn't difficult. If she agreed, would dating Finn be as easy?

"Of course, when the *Knights* make the playoffs, our agreement continues."

"Don't you mean *if* you make the postseason? Remember Chicago?" Erin hated to bring up a bad memory, but Finn gave her no choice. "How many times did your old team miss out on the playoffs?

"About half the time," Finn admitted through gritted teeth.

"What's the phrase for how you fared?" Erin tapped her chin. "One and done?"

"Ouch. Direct hit." Finn pretended to pull a dagger from his heart. "The *Knights* are different. We won't win one postseason game. We'll win them all."

"Your confidence is admirable," Erin said. "And a little sad. Don't ask me to console you when your dream becomes a nightmare."

"What I expect is for you to keep your word," Finn told her as he leaned close enough for her to see the flecks of silver in his eyes. "I want to look up and see you in the stands the day I help the *Knights* bring home another championship."

For Finn's sake, Erin hoped he was right. His dream was to win the *Super Bowl* and if that meant she had to suffer through the agony of watching as he was pummeled by the opposition, she was prepared to cheer him on—and suffer through every hit administered to his beautiful body.

Erin didn't want Finn to know her thoughts. If he did, he might try to talk her into attending a game or two during the regular season. Since he would fail, she saw no reason to get his hopes up.

"Time will prove one of us right," Erin said. "Maybe your season ends early. Maybe you win the Super Bowl. Either way, what happens after?"

"If you agree to my proposal, we date, exclusively—"

"Naturally," Erin interjected.

"Until the last second ticks off the clock to end the last game," Finn finished. "Then, the rest will be up to you."

"Meaning?" she asked.

"Simple," Finn told her. "We remain together, as a couple. Or I give you what you want. My sperm in a cup."

"In vitro fertilization and implantation are perfectly acceptable methods of conception." Erin sounded like a prim and proper science teacher. But she refused to let Finn make the process sound dirty.

"The advances made by science are great, Erin." Finn shrugged. "But why put yourself through an unnecessary procedure when you haven't even tried to conceive naturally."

"There's nothing *un*natural about invitro."

"You know what I meant." Finn held up his hands in defeat. "If you want to pick a fight to avoid the real issue, I won't play along."

"You're right," Erin admitted, surprising Finn and herself. "I need time to think. Can you give me some time?"

"I've waited years," Finn said. "A few more days won't kill me. Probably."

"Thank you."

With a nod, Finn headed toward the living room. Placing her hand on his arm, Erin stopped him. She had a question and now seemed like a good time to ask.

"When did I become more than a friend to you?" She picked her words carefully. "When did you start to want more?"

"The year you graduated from high school," he answered easily.

"You were only thirteen."

"Mm," he nodded. "I couldn't imagine having sex with anyone but you."

"That problem didn't last long," Erin snorted. "You moved on and slept with many, many women."

"No. I didn't," Finn told her without a trace of a smile.

"What are you talking about?" Erin laughed.

"I wanted you to be the first. And you will be." When Erin's mouth fell open, Finn shrugged. "I told you, I'm good at waiting."

At any second, Erin expected him to admit his bald-faced lie. Nothing he said made sense. As the seconds ticked away, the sincerity of Finn's expression didn't crack.

"What about all the women you dated?" she asked, her head spinning.

"We kissed. Fooled around a little. Nothing more." Finn took Erin's hand, flatting the palm over his chest. "I saved myself for you."

"You're...?" Erin swallowed. "A virgin?"

Finn's lips twitched. Then he snorted. Right in Erin's face. He bent at the waist, overcome with laughter. Trying to get himself under control—and failing miserably—he wiped the rolling tears of merriment from his face.

"Finally, you said the magic word. Virgin." Finn snorted. "I wondered if you'd give in. You did."

Erin wanted to slap the smug smile off Finn's mouth. The jerk. Instead, she tried to regain a bit of her dignity.

"I didn't believe you for a second," she said with an easy wave of her hand. "I just went along to see how far you'd carry the lie."

"All the way. To the hilarious end." Grinning, Finn shook his head. "You should have seen the look on your face. Priceless."

"I will retaliate," Erin warned. "When you least expect it, I'll go in for the kill."

"Whatever punishment you dole out will be worth the pain." Finn laughed again. "Why didn't I think to put my phone on record? The sound when you asked if I'm a virgin? What a perfect ringtone."

"Take your ringtone and stick it where the sun never shines, Finnegan."

Erin slid from the stool, prepared to stomp from the room.

"I was seventeen."

"Pardon?" Erin frowned. "You mean seventeen was the age when you had sex?"

"I won't name names," Finn said with a nostalgic smile. "A year younger than you lost your virginity."

"Whoa, cowboy," Erin scoffed. "Let's be clear. I didn't *lose* anything. My hymen was willingly relinquished."

"Christ," Finn sighed. "Why do doctors feel the need to be so graphically correct about every freaking bodily function? Yes, I know women are born with a hymen. But must I be reminded?"

"Second," Erin continued, thoroughly enjoying Finn's discomfort. "You couldn't possibly know where or when my first time occurred."

"I even know the who." Finn's mouth dipped into a frown. "Believe me, I'd happily have the knowledge wiped from my memory."

Amused, annoyed, and just a wee bit horrified, Erin grabbed the front of Finn's shirt before he could walk away.

"Tell me what you think you know," she demanded.

"Do you honestly expect me to reiterate the gory details?" Finn asked.

"Please," Erin said. "Since you can't possibly be right, I can't wait to hear whatever tale of fiction you concocted."

"When?" Finn began with a huff. "The night of your senior prom. Where? The backseat of a black Grand Torino."

"*Grand Torino*? Like the movie?" Erin had to laugh. "If the *who* in your story turns out to be Clint Eastwood, you can sell the tale to Hollywood."

"The who was Andy Driscoll," Finn said. "Still laughing?"

"No. But I might be sick." Amazed, Erin shook her head. "What makes you think that I would have sex with such a jerk?"

"The next fall, Andy bragged to everyone after football practice."

"And you believed him?" Erin rubbed her temples. "Of course, you did."

"He mentioned your heart-shaped birthmark," Finn said, his expression suddenly sheepish.

"The thing is located on the small of my back," Erin reminded him. "Hardly an intimate area."

"He lied." Finn sighed. "And you're angry."

"I'm disappointed," Erin corrected him. "How could you believe I'd do something so cliché? Sex in the backseat of a car? After the prom? Worse, with Andy Driscoll? He wasn't even my date that night."

"I was thirteen and hopped up on jealousy," Finn said in defense of himself. "Can't you give me a break?"

"Maybe." Erin was already three-quarters on the way to forgiving him. "If I asked, would you look Andy up and administer a retroactive smackdown?"

"Too late." Smiling, Finn shrugged. "The second we were off school property, I took care of the problem."

When Erin pictured Andy Driscoll the way he looked all those years ago, her eyes widened in surprise.

"You were thirteen. He was a senior and outweighed you by at least thirty pounds. Yet you managed to—"

"Beat the shit out of the asshole," Finn nodded. "He deserved every punch."

For herself and women everywhere, Erin agreed. She wrapped her arms around Finn's waist and hugged him close.

"Finny," she sighed. "My hero."

"Well." Awkwardly—a word she never associated with him—Finn patted Erin's back. "Okay."

"You're embarrassed," she said, her laugh tinged with amazement.

"A little." Finn shrugged. "I never planned for you to find out. Don't get me wrong, I'm thrilled to be proved wrong about Andy Driscoll. Still…"

"Real heroes prefer anonymity." Understanding, Erin nodded. "Don't worry. Your secret is safe."

"Thanks." Finn chuckled. He looked at his watch. "I need to get going."

"Training camp?" Erin rolled her eyes. "Silly question."

"First, I need to meet with Dad." Finn didn't look happy at the prospect.

"You finally answered one of his calls?" Erin asked, then sighed. "Again, the answer is obvious. He'll want money."

"He rarely gets in touch unless he's deep into a losing streak." Finn slipped on a black leather bomber jacket. Checking the pockets for his wallet and phone, he shrugged. "He's a gambler without much skill or luck. He freaking bleeds money."

"And expects you to give him a transfusion." Linking her arms with his, Erin walked Finn to the door. "I won't say to give him my best. I'd choke on the words."

"You could tell me to kick him to the curb." Finn's smile didn't reach his eyes. "Yet you never have. Not once."

"What would your advice be if Jerry Lennox were my father, not yours?"

"You want to trade? I'd take Walt off your hands in a heartbeat."

"No deal," Erin said with a firm shake of her head. "My dad is a one-of-a-kind gem."

"And mine is a pain in the—"

"Bank account?" Erin said in a lame attempt to inject a bit of humor. "Sorry. Bad joke."

"But accurate." Absently, Finn rubbed his neck. "You asked what advice I'd give you if our situations were reversed?"

"Mm," Erin nodded.

"I'd tell you to stop paying off his debts. Then, I hoped I'd understand when you did the opposite."

Finn didn't have a lot of family by blood. His Aunt Sheila, his mother's sister, passed away during his freshman year of college. A few distant cousins were all that remained, scattered here and there across the country.

Finn's image of Jerry Lennox as a loving, hard-working husband and father faded a little with each passing year. But that didn't make the memories any less real. Nor could he shake the hope that one day, the man who used to read him bedtime stories would pull his life together.

"Call if you want to talk," Erin said as the elevator doors opened. "Call if you need to hear my voice. You don't have to say a thing."

"What would I do without you?" Finn asked.

Erin looked into Finn's gray eyes. She brushed a non-existent piece of lint from his jacket and smiled.

"Luckily, you'll never have to find out."

CHAPTER THIRTEEN

FINN ONCE READ in a book that the love between a parent and child was sacrosanct and unbreakable. He was certain the author meant well. But as he looked at his father, the words rang hollow.

Nothing holy existed between Finn and Jerry Lennox. If love and hate were the same emotion, simply flipped on their side, he realized as he gazed into a pair of gray eyes the carbon copy of his own, he couldn't summon either feeling. Not anymore.

Finn was sorry to discover that obligation and guilt ran deep.

Jerry checked his phone for the third time as though afraid the money Finn transferred into his account might disappear.

"I'll pay you back, son," Jerry promised. "Won't take long until your old man is swimming in dough again."

Finn dismissed his father's words without a second thought. The money was gone, never to be seen again. He didn't keep a running tab. Even if he expected to receive remuneration—which he didn't—the chance he would get hit by lightning, five times in a row, while indoors, were better than his father keeping his word.

"Would you like something to eat?" Finn asked, alarmed at Jerry's gaunt appearance. Once tall and strong as an ox—at least in his memory—his father seemed small. Almost frail. "The steak sandwich here is good."

The waterfront restaurant was empty as the staff prepared for lunch. Friends with the owner, Finn asked if he could use one of the booths in the back for a private meeting. He never knew when his father might break into a long, sobbing rant about his sad life. The fewer people to bear witness, the better.

Jerry's gaze darted toward the exit. Finn recognized the look. Since his father had what he came for, he was anxious to be on his way.

"Won't the smell of meat offend your senses?" Jerry asked.

"No." Finn frowned. "Why?'

"You're a vegetarian. Right?" Jerry shrugged. "Thought I read you were a fanatic."

"I'm not," Finn said, surprised his father knew anything about his lifestyle. "Most of my friends are carnivores."

"Well, great. Friends are good." Jerry said with a vague smile. "Do you still hang out with that girl?"

Jerry never liked Erin. He thought she was a bad influence—ironic since she was the reason Finn got off his ass and nurtured the work ethic that led to his career in the NFL. Without football, he wouldn't have the money to pay his father's debts.

If anything, Jerry should worship the ground Erin walked on.

Since the last thing Finn wanted was to put the woman he loved in his father's crosshairs, he let the question pass without comment.

"Take care, Dad." For once, Finn decided to be the first to leave. "See you around."

"Sure. Right. Now that you're back in Seattle, we should get together," Jerry said in his usual vague way. "If not, I have your number."

To Finn's ears, his father parting words sounded like a threat *and* a promise.

"I WAS DUPED," Erin muttered. "Hornswoggled. Rooked. Thoroughly victimized."

"Don't exaggerate," Riley said with an amused snort. "I invited you to go shopping—one of your favorite activities. I didn't lie."

"What kind of shopping can we do on a football field?" Erin demanded.

"We aren't on the field," Riley pointed out. "We started in my office. Then, we stopped in the lounge for tea. Didn't you enjoy the scones and strawberry jam?"

"Bribery," Erin scoffed. "You know I have a weakness for anything buttery. Or sweet."

"The plan was to leave right after we finished our snack," Riley told her. "When I asked you to pick me up at work, I didn't expect to spend the next hour playing phone tag with three other executives."

Smiling, Riley flipped a long strand of dark hair over her shoulder. Dressed to explore some of Seattle's more trendy boutiques, her skirt and blouse were *Chanel*, her shoes, vintage *Oscar de la Renta*. Though always fashionable, when at work, she toned down the runway style for sleeker, more business chic ensembles.

"I admit you don't look like a typical owner of an NFL franchise," Erin said. "Still, you know how I feel about football."

"You don't like to watch the games. Look." Riley pointed out her office window toward the field. "Everyone out there plays for the *Knights*. Their goal is to protect Finn, not annihilate him."

When Erin winced, Riley swallowed a laugh.

"Sorry," she said. "Bad choice of words."

"Practice or the real thing, bodies hit bodies." Erin rubbed her arms to ward off a sudden chill. "You watch every game. How did you survive before Sean retired?"

"I love football," Riley shrugged. "I love Sean. If I spent any amount of time thinking he might get hurt, I would have gone crazy."

"I can compartmentalize my worry." Erin kept far from the window. "I simply pretend Finn is at the office."

"Impressive." Riley reached for her purse. "Let's go before the phone rings again."

The second they left Riley's office someone called her name. A tall, gangly young man dressed in tan chinos and a *Seattle Knights'* sweatshirt ran toward them, waving a clipboard.

"We should have snuck out the back way," Erin whispered.

"This is the back way," Riley said with a resigned sigh. "Unfortunately, everyone on staff knows my escape routes."

"The general manager needs to see you right away," the young man said in a breathless voice.

"Did Darcy say what the problem is about, Wade?"

"No," he shook his head. "All Ms. Stratham said was to ask you to meet her down on the field."

"Okay." Riley sent Erin an apologetic smile. "You want to come along?"

"Nope. No way." Erin shook her head. "They play football down there."

"What else would they do?" Wade asked with a puzzled frown.
"

"Besides," Erin continued. For some reason, she felt the need to find a new excuse. "When I have on a new pair of shoes, I never go near grass or dirt."

"Suede scuffs easily." Greed entered Riley's blue eyes when her gaze landed on Erin's feet. "*Ferragamo* pumps. Persimmon orange. Lucite heels filled with dried flowers. That part of the spring line isn't scheduled to hit the stores for another three months. I think I hate you."

"A lavender pair in your size will arrive at your house tomorrow." Erin gasped when Riley, bursting with excitement, dragged her into the elevator.

"Tell me more," her friend insisted.

"Nothing to tell. Not really. I asked my contact if she could find me another pair. Happy birthday six months early." Suddenly nervous, Erin watched the numbers as the elevator descended at an alarming rate. "Where are we going?"

"Don't panic." Riley patted her arm. "Keep your back to the field and everything will be fine."

"I'm taking back the shoes," Erin said as the doors opened.

"From here, you barely see anything," Riley assured her. "Oh, there's Finn. Nice catch."

Erin almost looked. She could shut her eyes, but her ears were another matter.

"Why is everything so loud?" she asked, wincing when she heard the unmistakable sound of a body hitting the ground with a discernible thud.

"He isn't getting up," Riley gripped Erin's hand. "Damn it. Where's the doctor?"

"I don't know." Wade turned a pale shade of green. "Is that blood gushing from Finn's neck?"

Erin's head whipped around.

"Wade!" Riley admonished. "Nothing is gushing from anyone."

Erin didn't care who was right. She needed to see for herself. She ran to the field. When her heels sank into the grass, slowing her progress, she ditched the shoes without a second thought.

Bodies, big, sweaty, and immovable, impeded her progress. She pushed, but her puny efforts were met with defeat.

"Move," Riley shouted. "Doctor coming through."

Whether it was the authority in Riley's voice or the promise of medical help for a fallen teammate that made the difference, Erin didn't care. The path cleared and five seconds later, she fell to her knees at Finn's side.

Dressed in a shirt that in bold letters declared him the team trainer, his upper lip was dripping with sweat. He held a thick piece of gauze to Finn's neck. Blood dripped around the edges.

"Who the hell are you?" he yelled when Erin would have pushed him out of the way.

"She's a doctor," Riley declared from a few feet away. "She's in charge."

"But—"

"Either help or get out of the way," Erin told the trainer. Then, she forgot he was there as years of experience and training kicked in.

Erin felt her panicked nerves calm. Ice water entered her veins.

"What caused the injury," she asked without looking up.

"Freak accident," the trainer told her. "A cleat caught him. Ripped a fucking gash three inches long."

Checking the wound, Erin breathed a sigh of relief when she found the wound was shallow and the blood didn't come from a grazed artery. She replaced the bloody gauze with a fresh bandage. She didn't think the injury was serious. But she needed to get him to a hospital to be certain.

"Finn? Can you hear me?"

"Erin?" Finn coughed. "Your timing sucks."

"Shh," she admonished. "Don't talk."

"First time I get you on a football field, and I take a cleat to the face," Finn wheezed. "Fucking dumb luck."

"The injury is on your neck, not your face."

"Thank God." His chuckle sounded weaker than Erin liked. "Any idea how much money I'd lose without my pretty face?"

"Millions." Erin shot a look at Riley. "Where's the ambulance?"

"Just arrived. Move back," Riley ordered. "Let the stretcher through."

"Don't leave me," Finn said, grasping Erin's hand.

"I won't." Reluctantly, she allowed the emergency medical technicians to take over. "Now, stop talking. We'll be at the hospital before you know it."

"Am I dying," he asked, groggy from loss of blood.

"Don't be such a drama queen." Erin climbed into the ambulance, taking his hand again. "Would I let you die?"

"No." Finn shook his head. "But after today, you might kill me."

Erin laughed, the sighed. Finn wasn't wrong. *Lord, she hated football.*

CHAPTER FOURTEEN

FINN WAS HOME.

For the first time since the accident happened, Erin allowed herself to breathe. Correction, she thought as she plugged a heating pad into the wall near the bed. For the first time since she saw Finn lying on the field, blood pouring from his neck, she was *able* to draw a proper breath into her lungs.

Tucking a blanket around Finn's shoulders, Erin found she couldn't take her eyes off him for more than a few seconds. As a doctor, she knew he was never seriously in danger. As his friend, the person who cared and watched over him for almost twenty years, all she could think about was how much worse his injury might have been.

The emergency was over, and she knew Finn would make a full recovery, yet her insides felt like Jell-O. When he needed her to stay calm, her hands were steady as a rock. Now, she couldn't stop shaking.

"I'm the one who lost a ton of blood," Finn said. "How come you're so pale?"

"I can't imagine."

"Sarcasm." Finn nodded, then winced. "If you can snap at me, I must be okay. If I were about to die, you'd be nice."

"I didn't snap," Erin rolled her eyes. She handed him a cup of lukewarm chicken broth and a straw. "And I told you before, and before that. You weren't at death's door. Not even in the neighborhood."

"Exactly what you would say to a dying man," he told her.

Erin fluffed a pillow before gently settling it behind Finn's head. "You're a lousy patient."

"Because I'm never sick." Finn sipped the broth. "I don't like the feeling."

"Do us both a favor," Erin said. "Never, ever again. Understand?"

"A cleat to the neck is the flukiest of fluke accidents." Finn yawned. He looked at the cup, then at Erin. "Did you slip me a mickey?"

The man was too smart for anyone's good—or hers. Since Finn refused to take a painkiller, he left her no choice but to dissolve one in his broth. Better he didn't know.

"A mickey?" Erin scoffed. "Who are you? Humphrey Bogart?"

"You want to be Lauren Bacall?" Finn winked.

"You aren't in any condition to fool around," Erin warned. "Save the weird sex games for another time."

"Weird is a stretch." Closing his eyes, Finn sighed and slipped lower onto his bed and under the covers. "But if you're in the mood for a sex game or two, give me twenty-four hours. I'm your man."

"You certainly are," Erin whispered.

"Hm?" Finn's eyes blinked open—just for a second. "Did you say something?"

"Your body needs time to recover," she told him. "Right now, sleep is the best medicine you can take."

"You *did* drug me." Finn frowned when Erin removed the cup from his hand. "Save the evidence. I plan to have the broth analyzed first thing in the morning."

"I'm a doctor, remember?" Erin asked with a smile. "I'll do the test."

"Perfect."

Finn's head lolled to one side. A moment later, his breathing normalized, and he was asleep.

At rest, with his eyes closed and face relaxed, Erin could almost believe Finn as the sweet, innocent boy she knew all those years ago. The thought was nice, and things would be easier if they could travel back in time.

What would be the point? Wouldn't they end up right where they were? Wasn't here, with Finn, exactly where Erin wanted to be?

With a sigh, Erin sat on the edge of Finn's bed, careful not to disturb him.

"You messed up the status quo, Finny." Erin couldn't help but smile. "After considerable thought, I can't say that I mind. Don't tell anyone. But I may like our new normal."

Erin shook her head, amazed at the feelings swirling inside of her as she looked at Finn. He wasn't a boy—hadn't been for a long time. But until recently, when she thought of him as a man, her pulse didn't pound with alarming speed. Nor did her blood race.

"Suddenly, I find eyes dropping to your lips. I wonder what your mouth would feel like against mine," Erin whispered. "What if you took me in your arms and I laughed because what's more ridiculous than the idea of us in a romantic relationship?"

Erin's gaze moved across Finn's familiar face and she felt a *very* unfamiliar tingle. She licked her lips then imagined him going the same.

Oh, boy. Mentally, she fanned herself. *Maybe the idea of them together wasn't as ridiculous as she once thought,* Erin decided.

"More times than I can remember, I watched you charm every woman in the room with a simple smile. I saw you seduce them and witnessed one or two leave your hotel room the next morning with smiles on their faces."

Erin frowned, not sure she liked where her musings led her.

"I never questioned how you were able to make a woman want you. But now I'd like to know." Erin took a shaky breath. "After all these years, how did you suddenly learn to make my heart flutter?"

Knowing she should leave him to rest, Erin hesitated a second, mulled the pros and cons, then gave into temptation and brushed a kiss across Finn's forehead.

An innocent enough gesture. Yet oddly erotic.

Calling herself a fool, she smiled, lifted her head, and found Finn's eyes wide open. Erin couldn't contain a gasp of surprise from escaping her lips.

"Remember what I told you?" Finn asked.

Caught in a trap of her own making, Erin shook her head. At that moment, she could barely remember her name.

"I said that I'd wait for you to…" His gaze dropped to her mouth. "What?"

"Make the first move," Erin whispered. He nodded.

"Consider it made."

Finn didn't wait for her to respond. He didn't give Erin time to think. He simply and thoroughly kissed her.

The was nothing tentative in Finn's approach. He was a man. Kissing a woman. And, *oh, God*, did he know exactly what he was doing. Not too hard, nor too soft. When he slid his tongue past her lips, it was smooth and unbelievably sexy. Like the sensation of silk gliding against satin.

Five more seconds and Erin would have sunk completely under Finn's spell. Her brain was a heart's beat from letting her body make all her decisions. She almost let herself forget why anything more than a kiss was a bad idea.

"I'm a doctor," Erin gasped.

"The sexiest, most beautiful, most desirable doctor ever put on the face of the earth," Finn said, punctuating each compliment with a lingering kiss to her cheek then the side of her neck.

Erin's well-developed selfish side turned her head, giving Finn and his magic lips better access to the sensitive skin just below her ear. Her toes curled when his teeth nipped, and his tongue soothed.

As Finn's fingers slid beneath the hem of her shirt, Erin's eyes flew open. *What was she doing?*

"Stop!"

"The magic word. Why now?" Finn asked, arms falling to his sides. When his head fell forward, he winced.

"There's your answer," Erin said, pulling in a ragged breath. She stood and moved several feet away. "You're hurt. You lost a lot of blood. You should be in the hospital. And I should know better."

"Because you're a doctor," Finn nodded. "Seemed like a strange form of dirty talk when you called out your profession. But I was ready to play along. Thank God I didn't yell, *I'm a football player.* I mean, how embarrassing, right?"

"I'm glad you can make a joke," Erin said with a shaky laugh. "I'm sorry."

"I'm not," Finn assured her.

"You need rest, not sex."

"My body tells a different story." Finn lifted the covers, his gaze moving down his body. "You heard the doctor. Down boy. Down!"

The guilt Erin felt for disregarding the fact that Finn was her patient first, her friend second, and a potential lover last, faded the moment Finn's infectious smile lit up his face. The knowing wink didn't hurt, either.

"I want you to get some sleep." Erin flipped the switch near the door sending the room into darkness except for the pale glow from the lamp near Finn's bed. "If you need anything, give me a call."

"I need you." Finn patted the other side of the bed. "I'll sleep better with you by my side."

"How many women have fallen for that line?" Erin asked.

"Is your answer no?" he asked.

"Emphatically."

"Since you're the first to hear the line, the number of women who fell is zero," Finn told her.

"I'll take your word." Erin laughed. "Goodnight."

"Erin."

"Yes?" She turned to face him.

"Earlier, when you thought I was asleep?" I heard everything." As though sensing her surprise and discomfort, Finn smiled. "Relax. You didn't say anything I didn't want to hear."

Erin wondered if her cheeks were red because her face felt on fire.

"You should have let me know you were awake," she chided him.

"And miss your confession? Not on your life." Finn shook his head, the light in his gray eyes gentle and loving. "I won't say the women before you meant nothing. That would be a lie and an insult to them and me."

Erin nodded. She might have suffered from a brief, relatively minor case of latent jealousy, but she would have been disappointed if Finn said anything else. Like her, everyone in his past helped make him who he was.

The details concerning his former liaisons, Finn could keep to himself. Erin didn't want to know. However, she would never want or expect him to forget.

"You're a good man, Finnegan Lennox."

"Glad to hear you use the word man." Finn sighed. "Seems like I've fought most of my life to make you see me as a fully grown adult."

"I haven't seen you as a boy for longer than I can remember," Erin assured him.

"I'm glad to know I make your heart flutter."

"Nothing I said when I thought you couldn't hear me is on the record," Erin told him. "Understand?"

"Too late. Every word is engraved. Right here." Finn tapped the spot on his chest directly over his heart.

Slightly annoyed, more than a little charmed, and frustrated that Finn could inspire both emotions with just a smile and a few sincerely delivered words, Erin turned to leave.

"I haven't finished."

Keeping her back to him, Erin waited.

"The fact that I make your heart flutter is a good thing," he said. "Wonder why?"

Despite everything that told her not to give him one more advantage, Erin nodded.

"Because, Erin Ashmore, I like you, too."

Without another word, Erin left the room, closing the door with a light click.

I like you.

Such a simple phrase. Short. To the point. And far more meaningful than a flowery, longwinded speech. Sometimes love was easy. Desire faded. Erin touched her lips and found a smile. When you liked someone, suddenly the world opened up to a myriad of endless possibilities.

CHAPTER FIFTEEN

"IF YOU CAN go to work, why can't I?" Finn asked for what seemed like one million and one times.

"I wasn't involved in a life-threatening accident," Erin explained as she tried to keep her patience.

Reminding herself that he led an active lifestyle and wasn't accustomed to having his movements curtailed helped. For a little while. By the third day, even her vaunted bedside manner was close to the breaking point.

"Tomorrow, you can resume your regular activities," Erin told him as she checked her bag to make certain she had everything she needed for the day. Remembering the way Finn's wily brain operated, she quickly added, "Within reason."

"I can go for a walk?" he asked.

"Yes," Erin nodded.

"Run?"

"A few miles, sure," she said.

"How about if I hit the gym?"

"A light workout," Erin warned. "Nothing heavy until your stitches are removed."

"What about practice?" Finn smiled his most charming smile. "Please, doctor."

"Football?" Was he crazy? "No. Absolutely not."

Erin almost added never but realized her authority as his doctor had its limits. As his girlfriend? Since they still hadn't come to terms with the change in their relationship, she would be on shaky ground if she played that singular card.

Either way, Erin would never ask Finn to give up football. He loved the game, excelled on the field, and made way too much money for her to ask him to quit. It was one thing when he was thirteen and she was still naïve and arrogant enough to believe her word was law. Now, she accepted his decisions—mostly.

Finn's life, Finn's choice.

"When can I get back on the field?" Finn asked.

Erin could see the frustration, the desperation, in his eyes. And, despite her aversion to the game, her heart went out to him. She couldn't imagine a day when the dictates of her body, and someone else's judgment, stopped her from practicing medicine. Just the thought made her shudder.

"I consulted with the Knights' team doctor. He agrees that it would be best if you skipped the last two preseason games."

Certain Finn would explode, Erin waited for the eruption. And waited. And waited.

"Aren't you going to argue with me?" she asked when he opened the refrigerator and calmly poured himself a glass of orange juice. "You've had plenty of time to think up a grocery list of reasons why you should be allowed to play."

"I'll be ready for opening day?" Finn asked. "You'll give me the green light?"

"Unless some unforeseen complication arises, you'll be good to go," Erin assured him.

Finn set the glass on the counter, crossed to Erin, and took her in his arms.

"Thank you,' he said.

Taken off guard, Erin hugged him back.

"I want what's best for you."

"I know," Finn nodded.

"If you suited up before you were ready, you'd risk missing more time," Erin explained even though Finn didn't ask. "If you sacrifice a few meaningless games now, you can start the season at one hundred percent both mentally and physically."

"Right."

Erin didn't understand the reason, but she felt close to tears.

"What would I do if something happened?" She sniffled. "I would never forgive myself."

"Because you like me." Finn sounded slightly smug.

"Because I'm your doctor," Erin corrected. Then added, "And yes. Because I like you. Jerk."

"One more question." Finn nuzzled her neck, his breath hot against her skin. "When can we make love?"

At least Finn had his priorities straight, Erin scoffed. Football, then sex. Where she fell in the hierarchy, she couldn't say. Since she had the final say on when he played and because she was the object of his desire, she decided to put herself at the top of his list.

If Finn had other ideas, too bad. She didn't ask.

"When we have sex—"

"Make love," Finn insisted.

Erin rolled her eyes. And she thought she liked to argue. Lately, Finn had her beat by a mile.

"Don't get lost in semantics," Erin told him.

"The difference between having sex and making love may be slight in your mind. Not in mine." Finn looked her straight in the eye, his gaze steady. "I've had sex. I enjoy sex. Sex is one of my favorite activities. I've never made love. Have you?"

"No." Erin could think of no reason to hem or haw. "I haven't."

"Good." A smile lit Finn's face and traveled straight to his eyes. "You can be my first. I'll be yours."

"Considering the subject matter, I won't say that you look like a little kid who just received his favorite treat," Erin laughed. "But if the shoe fits…"

Leaning against the kitchen countertop, Finn pulled Erin between his legs. He raised her hands to his lips.

"When?" he asked, kissing each fingertip with a slow thoroughness she had to admire. "Set a date."

"A week from Friday at seven-fifteen."

Finn frowned. Did his accident impair his ability to discern sarcasm? Erin swallowed a smile.

"We need to wait a whole seven days?" Finn sighed. "If you're worried that I can't perform, don't. All the parts are working. If you need proof, meet me in the shower tomorrow morning."

"A lot of men wake with an erection. It's perfectly normal but isn't indicative of how he would perform in a sexual situation," Erin informed him, shifting from potential lover into doctor mode. Then, she shifted back. "In other words, when the chips are down, you might strike out, slugger."

"Impossible," Finn said with a man's typical arrogance. "My success rate is one hundred percent."

Erin snorted. Why, even when slightly obnoxious, was he so darn cute?

"Let's play the timeline by ear," she said. "Unless you're okay with simply lying on the bed like my personal sex toy. If so, we can have a go anytime you like."

"You think you're funny," Finn huffed. "Trust me, you're not."

"Maybe a little?" With a teasing light in her eyes, Erin's gaze dropped to Finn's crotch. "Or is little a word I shouldn't use?"

"You want to find out?" Finn reached for the waistband of his sweatpants. "In about five seconds, you'll never put me and little in the same sentence again."

"Big talk," Erin snorted. But just in case he was serious, she swatted away his hands.

"Big," he nodded. "Exactly."

"I'm leaving."

Erin picked up her jacket. With Finn's help, she slid her arms into the sleeves. One second a twit, the next a gentleman. Was it any surprise that her heart teetered on the precipice of falling?

Erin didn't need a nudge or even a tremor to send her over the edge. She'd come to terms with the fact that love, the kind between a woman and a man, was inevitable. What she needed was a little more time for her head to catch up with the rest of her.

"The time will come. Right?" Finn asked as she settled her feet into a pair of sky-blue patent leather pumps. "We will make love."

Since forever, Finn always needed answers—often before the dust from his questions had time to settle. More impatient than pushy, he made up his mind quickly and couldn't understand why others weren't as decisive.

Finn seemed to forget that he had years to come to terms with his feelings for her. What was comfortable to him felt new and a little frightening to Erin. His patience was admirable, all things considered.

Didn't Finn deserve to know he wasn't alone? That she wanted him—if not for as long—as much as he wanted her.

"Finn?"

"Yes?"

The eager, puppy quality in Finn's eyes was almost too adorable for words. So, she didn't speak. Instead, Erin simply nodded. As the elevator doors closed, the sound of his whoop of joy met her ears.

"Ah, Finn," Erin laughed, her heart swelling with wonder. "I think I love you."

CHAPTER SIXTEEN

ERIN DIDN'T GET the chance to sleep in very often. Her busy schedule meant she wasn't allowed the luxury. Even when she had a few extra minutes to spare, her internal clock woke her at the same time each morning.

Though Erin wasn't due at the hospital until after ten o'clock and she had another doctor to cover any emergencies at her clinic, this morning wasn't any different from every other. Before the first ray of light peeked over the Cascade Mountains, her eyes were open.

"Warm," Erin sighed, snuggling under the covers. "Where's the rule that says I can't relax for a few minutes. Or an hour. I've earned the right."

Finn didn't get the message. Less than ten minutes passed before a knock sounded on her door. Before she could yell for him to get lost, he was in her room, bursting with the kind of energy reserved for a six-year-old child hopped up on too much sugar.

Or a grown man forced to put a hold on his normally active lifestyle.

"Time to go for a run."

Erin opened one eye, just enough to find a pair of long, legs blocking her view. She had two options. Punch him in the nuts—so close, so tempting—or roll over and pretend he didn't exist.

As Erin turned her back to him, Finn didn't know how he almost ended up on the receiving end of the kind of pain no man wants to experience.

"You can join me for a run," Finn said, undeterred. "Or I can join you under the covers."

"Knock yourself out," Erin muttered. With a sigh, she sat up, glaring at him through a curtain of blonde hair. "I warn you, I'm not in the mood."

"I'll change your mind." Finn pushed his jogging shorts down an inch. Then another. "What do you say?"

"You don't threaten a doctor with nudity," Erin scoffed. "Do you have any idea how many dicks I've seen? Big ones, small ones."

"You've never seen mine," Finn told her with a smile.

"Fair point. I hope to. Soon." Erin sighed. "But not today. Give me ten minutes. I'll meet you downstairs."

"I don't know if I feel disappointed or excited. What the hell, I'll decide later," Finn said with a chuckle. He patted Erin's leg. "Don't be late."

"Screw you."

"You will." Finn winked. "But not today."

Alone, Erin pulled the covers over her head, mulling odds that if she didn't show up, Finn would leave without her. Knowing him, she decided the math wasn't worth the effort. With a resigned sigh, she rolled from the bed.

"No one should be that chipper so early in the morning," she muttered and headed for the bathroom.

FINN'S IDEA OF a run meant a leisurely first mile to warm his muscles and get his blood flowing followed by a six-mile sprint, two more at a slower pace, and finally, a flat-out race to the finish.

With Erin along, he let her set the pace. Rather than worry about building his cardio strength, he was content to take in the crisp morning air and enjoy the novelty of having her by his side.

"Aren't you glad I asked you to join me?"

"Whether you asked or bullied is open to interpretation," she said.

Erin breathed in and out with ease, allowing her to talk without effort. She wasn't concerned about showing off or worried if she held Finn back. She knew her limits and was happy to stay within her boundaries.

"Mornings are the best time for a run. The earlier the better." Finn looked around. "No one's around to get in the way."

"Do people bother you when you're out?" Erin asked.

"The worst is when someone decides to run with me." Finn sighed. "Not close enough to be considered an invasion of my space, but another person's grunting and huffing tend to break my concentration."

"Is my breathing too loud?" Erin laughed.

"You're fine," Finn assured her. "Mostly, I get a lot of pointing and staring. And cameras. Why would anyone want a picture of me sweating?"

"The fact that you don't know, is adorable."

"What?" Finn frowned. "Tell me."

"Not that your ego needs a boost, but what the heck?" Erin ran her eyes over him, top to bottom and back again. "A tall, fit, beautifully muscled man covered in perspiration is sexy."

"I don't find sweaty women particularly sexy," he said. Glancing at Erin, he had a change of heart. "Maybe *one* woman."

"Maybe?" Erin shook her head. "I'm crushed. I thought you were hot for me no matter what."

"I am. Want proof?"

Finn grabbed Erin's wrist, pulling her behind a large oak tree that shielded them from the street and passing traffic. Pressing forward until her back was flat against the column of smooth, white-colored bark, he covered her mouth with his.

The first time they kissed, Finn wasn't at his best, despite how he tried to convince Erin. Woozy from the loss of blood and slightly loopy from the pain meds she tricked him into swallowing, his memory felt more dreamlike than real.

Finn spent too many years fantasizing about Erin in his arms. He wanted—needed—a dark, sweet, thirst-quenching dose of reality.

"More."

Certain he must have said the word aloud, Finn was surprised and delighted when he realized Erin was the culprit. *More*? He would give her all she wanted. Every inch of him. Every breath he had to take. If she asked him for the moon, he'd die trying to hand over her wish.

"You taste like—"

"Toothpaste?" Erin said with a laughing gasp. Eyes sparkling brighter than any star, she slid her fingers through Finn's hair until her hand cupped the back of his head. "You, too."

Finn bit her tongue, hard enough to get her attention. When Erin moaned, his eyebrows lifted in surprise. His lady enjoyed a spark of pain? Interesting. He filed the new-found knowledge away for future reference.

"I was going to say that you taste like peppermint." Finn swiped the corner of her mouth. "Much more romantic."

"Save the romance for another time," Erin growled. She ran her free hand up the inside of his thigh. "Just freaking kiss me."

Finn was happy to oblige. He always wondered how Erin would respond to his touch. When he was younger and green as grass, his imagination didn't take him far. Now, with a world of experience to judge by, he was thrilled. Ecstatic.

When Finn brushed his fingers across the nape of her neck, Erin sighed. When he ran his tongue over the curve of her ear, she moaned. And when he cupped her breast, resenting the layers of her jacket, shirt, and bra that stood between her skin and his, she made a sound of pleasure deep in her throat that made every nerve in his body stand up and say thank you.

If heaven was a place on earth, the location was in her arms. The name? Erin.

Finn couldn't believe they had to stop, but Erin would lose her mind if a video of them making out popped up on *YouTube*. Just as things were getting interesting, Finn moved Erin's hand from between his legs.

"We're on the street. In public. Where people can see," Finn reminded. "You aren't wearing face paint and a wig this time."

"So?" she asked in a raspy voice that shook Finn's resolve to do the right thing.

Why here? Why now? Why was he foolish enough to start something he couldn't finish? Because you never dreamed Erin would go up like a room filled with fireworks. Thrilled that he was the match who lit her fuse, now was not the time or place to find out just how hot they could burn.

"You're killing me," Finn groaned. He trapped Erin's roaming fingers over her head. "We're five minutes from home. Three if we haul ass."

Finn expected Erin to stop. Pull away. Come to her senses. He didn't think she would grab his hand and run. He laughed. The woman he knew almost better than himself had a few surprises up her sleeve. And he approved. Whole-heartedly.

"You're fast," Finn declared when two and a half minutes later, Erin punched the security code into the front door keypad.

"I was motivated," she said.

Grabbing the front of Finn's jacket, Erin dragged him into the apartment. She reached for his shorts, ready to rip them from his body—he hoped—then stopped.

"The condoms are upstairs."

"Why?" Finn asked in a mournful voice.

"I've never been impatient enough to need them down here." Laughing, Erin jumped into his arms the way she had at the airport, arms around his neck, her long legs wrapped around his waist. "You inspire me, Finny."

"Hold on," he said after a long, hot kiss. "You haven't seen anything yet, beautiful."

Finn took the stairs three at a time. He shouldered his way into Erin's room and tossed her on the bed. As he unzipped his jacket, her phone rang. She froze, he cursed.

"Well, fuck," Erin said as she looked at the screen.

"Did you just say the f-word?" Finn laughed, or maybe he cried. Between the sweat and mounting frustration, he couldn't be certain.

"Sometimes darn just doesn't cut it." Erin left her phone on the bed and raced to the bathroom. She left the door open. "I have five minutes to shower and get dressed."

"Another woman in labor?" Finn asked, raising his voice over the sound of running water.

"Babies are funny," Erin called back. "Doesn't matter that they were created when mommy and daddy had made love. By the time they're ready to leave the womb, sympathy goes out the door for our bodily needs. Childbirth waits for no man, woman, or sex life."

"Nice speech," Finn said as she rushed from the bathroom in nothing but a towel. He averted his eyes, not out of modesty for her or embarrassment on his end. Right now, too much bare Erin was more than he could handle.

Two minutes later, Erin emerged from the closet. Her hair was wet, but she was fully dressed. When Finn took her bag and followed her to the elevator, she tried to stop him, but he had other ideas.

"I'll shower after you leave," he told her as they rode together to the parking garage. "I'm in the mood to see your face every second I can."

"Aw." Erin took his hand. "I'd apologize for the interruption…"

"Part of who you are," Finn shrugged. "My Erin is a doctor. Quick question though."

"Hm?" she asked, frowning when her phone rang again. She checked the screen and waved for him to continue.

"At some point if *you* get pregnant, way, way in the future." When she raised an eyebrow, he shrugged. "I have hope you'll pick me *and* a baby. Anyway. You can't run to the hospital every five minutes when you have a bun in the oven."

"I'll take a leave of absence, naturally." Erin's phone rang again. She shrugged and answered. "Mom."

"Your mother?" Finn mouthed the question.

When Erin nodded, he felt guilty, as though they were caught red-handed doing something they weren't supposed to do.

"Sorry I couldn't pick up before." Erin carried on the conversation as she walked to her car. "Finn and I were just about to have sex."

"What?" Finn yelled, then quickly lowered his voice, worried Erin's mother would hear. "Are you out of your mind?"

"Don't worry," Erin said, her lips twitching as Finn almost had a heart attack. "We were interrupted. We didn't even get naked."

Finn knew he would never be able to look Erin's mother in the face again. The woman trusted him to keep her daughter safe, not rut on top of her.

Not that Finn planned to keep his hands off. But parents, no matter how close you were to them, should be kept in the dark about such matters.

"Oh. I guess that wasn't Mom on the phone," Erin said as she hung up. "Just a robocall recording. My mistake."

"A mistake?" Finn scoffed. "My heart almost stopped."

"You lied about your so-called virginity. I lied about telling Mom we plan to have sex." With a satisfied smirk, Erin slid behind the wheel of her car.

"Evil," Finn hissed.

"Payback," Erin countered. "You were warned."

Standing back, Finn watched as Erin drove up the ramp, paused at the top, and pulled into the street. He chuckled and headed back to the apartment.

Were they even? Finn wasn't. Seemed to him that Erin took her joke on him to another level. She had a quick and devious mind.

Finn laughed. No wonder he loved her.

CHAPTER SEVENTEEN

ERIN LET HERSELF into the apartment. The clock on the wall read a quarter to ten. She tried to get away from the hospital at a reasonable hour, but some days, circumstances worked against her.

The delivery went without a hitch. After a short but intense hour of labor, mother and daughter were doing fine. With two boys at home, the little girl was the final addition to a loving family. No more babies, Mom declared. Dad was on board with the decision.

The young father brought up the possibility of a vasectomy. When his wife asked Erin's opinion, she told them that where such decisions were concerned, she was Switzerland—neutral.

A life-changing decision, it was something the couple needed to discuss on their own, at a date somewhere in the future. After the hormones settled and the excitement and exhaustion of their daughter's birth weren't foremost in their minds.

If the husband still wanted details on a vasectomy, Erin promised to recommend a doctor they could trust.

The rest of Erin's day was spent on her least favorite part of her profession. Paperwork, board meetings, and schmoozing donors. Most of the time she was lucky. The hospital employed someone in charge of fundraising.

However, when someone consented to gift a large sum of money, they expected to be wined, dined, and entertained by *Seattle Generals'* most prominent doctors. Flattered that she was considered a star by her peers, Erin argued that the revenue she brought in should have been enough to exempt her from even the smallest amount of glad-handing. The administration didn't agree.

Three of four times a year, Erin found herself unable to get out of drinks and dinner. However, when the chief of staff tried to pressure her into bringing Finn along, she put down her foot. He had nothing to do with the hospital. She wouldn't let anyone trot him out like a show pony or use his celebrity to their advantage.

"Hello."

Erin jumped, startled by Finn's voice. She looked around the darkened living room and found him sitting on her favorite overstuffed chair, enjoying her favorite view of the city.

Erin wiggled her toes and smiled. The simple act of removing her shoes was the best part of her evening. Until now. She joined Finn in the chair and snuggled close. *Now*, she was happy. When his arm went around her shoulders and his lips brushed her temple, the problems of her day faded like the morning dew in the sun's warm glow.

"Did you have a good time," Finn asked.

"I did not."

Shaking her head, Erin lay her head on his arm. The soft cotton of his shirt warmed by his skin was a welcome balm. Better than any amount of aromatherapy. Instantly, her spirits rose.

"Want to talk about it?"

"Talk about what?" Erin smiled. "I already forgot everything that happened before I walked in and found you."

"Good answer." Again, he kissed her temple. Then her nose. Finally, he placed a sweet kiss on her lips. "You should get some sleep."

"Not tired," Erin said, surprised to discover she spoke the truth.

"Would you like some wine? A snack? I know you have a stash of junk food squirreled away somewhere."

"Nope." She shook her head. "There is something I want."

"Tell me." Finn waited. "Anything."

"You."

"Are you sure?" he asked.

Erin detected a slight tremor in Finn's voice, a hint of vulnerability. She understood. When you wanted something so much, when the moment came to achieve your desire, sometimes your luck seemed too good to be true.

"I may take longer than you to make up my mind," she said. "But once I do, have you ever known me to doubt my decision?"

"No." Finn shook his head. "Never."

Erin straddled his hips, the skirt of her dress riding high on her thighs. The flash of surprise in his gray eyes was followed by a spark of desire that every woman dreamed of seeing at least once in her life.

Without raising a sweat, Finn could have his choice of women. They fell at his feet. And yet, he wanted her. The knowledge was heady.

"I'm not the most beautiful woman in the world," Erin said as she took in the features of his handsome face.

"You're wrong. Doesn't happen often." Finn shook his head as though amazed. "But when you make a mistake, it's a doozy."

Erin ran her thumb over Finn's bottom lip. She smiled when his teeth took a bite.

"I'm opinionated."

"Compliant women are boring," Finn countered.

"I eat junk food when no one's around to see."

Erin didn't think the consumption of a few *Ding Dongs* was a sin, but she was running out of bad things to say about herself. She was certain her faults were many but listing them at the spur of the moment wasn't as easy as she might have imagined.

"Tell me something I don't know," Finn insisted.

"Impossible," Erin sighed. "You know all my secrets."

"And you know mine." Finn cupped her chin, his fingers gentle against her skin. "What point do you want to make?"

"Before we go any further, I wanted to give you one last chance to back out."

135

As Erin spoke the words, she had a thought. *Let him back out? Are you crazy?* Thank goodness Finn felt the same.

"Most of my life, I ran towards you," he said. "Now, inches from the goal line, you expect me to fumble?"

"A sports metaphor?" Erin rolled her eyes.

"I'm an athlete," Finn shrugged. "What did you expect"

Erin gasped when his hand closed around her calf. Finn's expression didn't change, but she detected a flare of heat in his eyes.

"Don't distract me," she warned. When he merely shrugged and moved his hand to her knee, Erin focused. "A fumble is unintentional. If I'm the ball—God forbid—you might want to drop me on purpose. Throw me away because I'm not worth the effort."

"Never," Finn scoffed. "Why would you suggest such a thing?"

"Guess I'm not as confident as I seem."

"Good." His lips hovered close to hers. "Puts us firmly in the same boat."

Finn was exactly what Erin never knew she wanted. Now that he was here, in her arms, she couldn't get enough.

"Slowly," she urged. Lightly, she touched the bandage on his neck. "I don't want to hurt you."

"I won't break," he said.

"Neither will I," she assured him.

"Good to know. First thing, let's get rid of these." Finn tugged on her panties, pulled again, then with a frustrated growl, ripped them from her body. He held the scraps of material up for her to see. "Oops."

"I have others," she said. "What's the second thing?"

"Guess."

Finn's hand moved between her legs. One finger, then two slid into past her slick folds, into her body. Erin's head fell back with a gasping sigh. No doubt. She was a big fan of the second thing.

"Unzip your dress," Finn told her. "Please."

"You know I'm a sucker for good manners." Erin did as he asked. With a shrug of her shoulders, the silky material fell past her arms, pooling at her waist.

"So much better than my dreams," Finn said as his mouth closed around the tip of her breast, the lace of her bra more of a temptation than a deterrent.

Erin breathed in his scent. Spice. Citrus. Finn. The combination made her dizzy. His touch made her ache. His mouth made her crazy.

"The condoms are upstairs?" Finn asked.

Erin, swept away by passion, almost told him not to worry. She was on the pill. But she was at her most fertile time of the month and the last thing she wanted was for Finn to think she deliberately used him to get pregnant. They were in too good a place to let a mistake and a misunderstanding ruin everything.

"Pause. Just for a minute," she said. "Let's go to bed and continue when we get there."

"Soon." Finn flipped Erin around. Positioning himself between her legs, he slid to his knees. "After I take care of you."

Magic. Erin could think of no other way to describe what Finn did for her. She threaded her fingers through his hair the strands silky and smooth against her skin. Urging him on, her grip tightened as he brought her close to her release with a skilled combination of his lips, tongue, and hands.

Just when Erin thought she could take no more, he eased up, leveled her out, then pushed to and past her limit. Resting her foot on his shoulder, her toes pressed into firm flesh and supple muscles.

"Stay with me," Finn told her, the hot swirl of his breath adding another layer of intensity. "Let go. Now."

Erin didn't fall, she hurtled over the edge as the orgasm shot through her body like a jolt of liquid lightning. She gasped Finn's name as she spun out of control only to land, safely, sated, in his arms.

"You are..." Erin gasped for breath. "Good."

"I'll take good," Finn laughed, lifting in his arms. "But my goal is great. Spectacular. Stupendous."

"Don't get ahead of yourself." Erin stretched before wrapping her arms around his neck. "Convince me. One orgasm at a time."

"I'll do my best."

Finn stopped at the top of the stairs, looked right, then left, and finally headed toward Erin's bedroom.

"You have the jetted tub," he explained. He set her feet on the floor. "For later."

"Because you only take showers," Erin wiggled her dress past her hips. When Finn stared, she looked down, following the path of his gaze. "What?"

"Just enjoying the view," he said. "If you ever doubt how beautiful you are, look in the mirror."

Finn didn't understand. Erin could look all she wanted but she would never see herself through his eyes. Then again, when she watched him watching her, everything she needed to know was written on his face. She knew without a doubt that he believed she was beautiful.

"Bra, off." Finn divested her of the lacy garment in a practiced flick of his wrist. He backed her up until her legs hit the mattress and gave her a gentle push. "You, on the bed."

"Your turn." Erin propped her head on her hand. "Clothes, off."

"Whatever the lady wants, the lady gets," Finn said with a flirty wink.

There wasn't much of him Erin hadn't seen. Swim trunks didn't hide a lot. However, until now, she hadn't been privy to the entire package—so to speak. Almost naked Finn wasn't the same as the man without a stitch of clothing to cover the interesting parts.

"Okay, I was wrong," Erin said, licking her suddenly dry lips. "Every penis is not created equal. And you, my friend... Wow!"

"Like what you see?" Finn asked. When Erin nodded, he grinned. He joined her, rolled over, and covered her body with his. "Now what are you going to do with me?"

Erin placed a hand on each side of Finn's face, stared into his eyes, and kissed him. Her moves weren't practiced. She didn't think about how to get from point A to B. With him, she didn't think at all. The only thing that mattered was making him as happy as he made her.

"I found the condoms," Finn said.

Yes, Erin laughed, he made her happy. In so many ways.

"Did I say something funny?" he asked as he tossed the foil wrapper away.

"You, my dear, Finn, are pure joy." Erin kissed him again, lingering over the pleasurable task.

"Remember what you said would happen the next time I piss you off?"

"Just shut up and make love with me."

"Love?" Finn's eyes lit up.

"More than sex," Erin said, not ready to put a name to her feelings. "Okay?"

Finn kissed the tip of one breast before he moved to the other. Erin sighed. Everything he did felt right. Her hands gripped his hips, her fingers tightening as her desire escalated once again.

At times, passion was ephemeral, easily lost with one wrong move or an errant thought. Finn kept Erin focused with his white-hot caresses and his smoldering kiss. She wasn't required to analyze or dissect. The only thing he required was her complete participation.

Mind and body. Both were his. *She* was his. And he was hers.

"Want to go for a ride," Finn asked with a mischievous smile.

He lay with his back against the headboard, Erin facing him. Waiting, patient yet coiled with passion, he watched as she slowly lowered herself, joining their bodies until they were one.

"You set the pace," he told her, his hands splayed over her hips.

Finn's fingers bit into her flesh. If he left a few bruises, Erin didn't care. Pleasure far outweighed the pain.

Erin pressed into him, rose then fell. They found a rhythm, unique, and powerful. Finn gripped the base of her neck, pulling her into a kiss. His breath melded with her, each groan, each sigh, music to her ears.

When Finn tensed, Erin increased her speed. His hips lifted, thrust, and froze as he shouted her name. A moment later, she followed, soared in a burst, then slowly floated back to earth.

"Perfect," Finn whispered.

Erin was too tired to do anything but smile when he tucked the covers around them and settled her into his arms.

"I'm not finished," he told her.

"Neither am I," Erin said as she brushed a kiss, a promise, over his shoulder. She didn't have the energy to reach any higher. "We've just begun."

CHAPTER EIGHTEEN

FINN LOOKED IN the mirror and frowned at his reflection. Everything appeared to be in place. Yet, something felt off.

"Does my tie seem wonky?" Finn asked Erin. "I can't seem to get the knot right."

"The tie is perfect," Erin assured him as she secured the back of her earring. "You're perfect. Why are you so fidgety tonight?"

"I'm not. Exactly."

Erin batted away his hand when Finn would have removed his tie and started over again. Smiling, she smoothed her fingers over his cheek before running her hand down the length of emerald green silk around his neck.

"Are you nervous about tonight?" A teasing glint entered her blue eyes. "Relax, Finny. Mom and Dad won't guess that you defiled their little girl just by looking at us."

"Don't joke." Finn let out a shaky breath. "I've known your parents most of my life. Back in college, do you know how many times your father mentioned how grateful he was that you had a man living in the house to keep you safe?"

"No," Erin said. "How many times?"

"Again," Finn told her. "Not funny."

"I agree." Her expression turned dark. "I didn't need someone to protect me. I never have."

"You missed the point." Finn sighed. "Do you know how proud I was when he called me a man? I was eighteen. You thought I was still a kid. My Dad barely thought of me at all. But your father? He shook my hand. Put his trust in me. Man, to man."

"I see." Erin nodded. "You think my father will lose respect for you when he discovers his thirty-six-year-old daughter is no longer pure? Worse, that you, the man he trusted to keep me safe, are the one who devirginized me?"

Finn grabbed his jacket and stomped from the bedroom. For good measure, he slammed the door. Erin caught up at the bottom of the stairs. She took his hand.

"Come on, Finn," she said, squeezing his fingers. "Lighten up. As far as my family is concerned, we're friends and roommates. Same as always. Even if by some stretch of the imagination, they found out, what do you think Dad will do? Beat you up?"

"I would in his place."

"Dad is sixty-three years old and has a bad back. He's in no condition to hit anyone." Erin's lips twitched. To add insult to injury, she snorted. "My brothers on the other hand? They'll probably knock the tar out of you."

Finn straightened his shoulders, pulling himself up to his full, six-foot-three-inch height. In the family hierarchy, he would take whatever Erin's father wanted to dish out. Siblings were another matter. They might be older by almost a decade, but pride dictated that he didn't put up with any of their shit.

"I can take your brothers."

"Don't tell Alan and Cory that," Erin warned as Finn helped her on with her jacket. "As lawyers, they take everything as a challenge."

"I should let them beat me up," Finn decided. "Your dad can watch. And your mom. If she wants."

Shaking her head, Erin buttoned Finn's royal blue cashmere overcoat—her gift to him on this incredibly special day. She took hold of the lapels and waited until she had his full attention.

"Today is your birthday. If I had my way, we would have stayed in, had a low-key celebration—the way you prefer." She shrugged.

"Mom likes to make a fuss and since you can never say no to her, we will have dinner, eat some cake, and come home."

"But—" Finn swallowed. "How can I eat your mom's food when I've done things to her daughter?"

"Things?" Erin laughed—hard. "I'll explain that I thoroughly enjoyed every second. Then reciprocated with *my* things. Just this morning. My mouth. A couple of ice cubes. A good time was had by all."

The memory was vivid and fresh. And Finn was only human. He felt a rush of blood from his brain to his dick. His eyes found Erin, smirking.

"I hate you," he muttered.

"GREAT GAME LAST Sunday." Cory Ashmore grinned and slapped Finn on the back. "Seven games, twelve touchdown receptions. Impressive. Think you have a shot at setting the single-season record?"

"Who knows," Finn said. "Personal stats are great, but my job is to help the *Knights* win games. The rest is gravy."

"Come on," Erin's brother scoffed. "Drop the party line for just a minute. You'd kill to win the league's most valuable player award. Hell, in your shoes, I would."

"Wouldn't anyone?" Alan asked. He was the oldest Ashmore sibling. He possessed the same stocky build and dark hair as his brother and father. Erin's fair looks and slender frame came directly from her mother.

"I know the NFL leans toward quarterbacks for the MVP award," Cory continued. "And Levi Reynolds is killing it under center this year. But you're the superstar, man. Once the ball is snapped all eyes are on you."

Finn was used to talking football at parties. When you played the game, everyone—non-sports fans included—seemed to assume it was the only subject you knew.

People would be surprised by how diverse the topics were when players socialized. Art. Music. Literature. Family. The latest movies. Politics—if alcohol wasn't involved. Sure, they talked football; the game was their bread and butter. But not exclusively.

Finn and his brethren were athletes. They were also human beings with other things on their minds.

"Give Finn a break. He spends all day and part of his nights either playing or studying football." Erin jabbed Cory in the ribs— a typical little sister move. "For a few hours, can't you talk about something else?"

Alan and Cory looked crestfallen. They were the only ones among their friends who knew a professional football player—and one of the best in the game to boot. Seemed like a waste not to pump Finn for as much inside information as possible.

Finn would have loved to clear his brain of x's and o's for one evening. But these were Erin's brothers. From the time he was a kid, they treated him like one of the family.

Just because Finn's name was mentioned on *SportsCenter* and his face graced the covers of a few magazines, he didn't want the Ashmore clan to think success had gone to his head.

"I don't mind," Finn told Erin.

"Well, I do. I declare a moratorium on any more football talk for the rest of our visit." Erin gave her brothers a warning glare. "Understood?"

When Erin walked away, sending one more pointed look over her shoulder, Cory shivered.

"Little sister barely weighs a buck fifteen," he said. "Why is she so damn scary?"

"Hell, if I know." Alan scratched his head. "Finn? You spend the most time with her. Any ideas?"

Smiling, Finn shrugged and remained silent. Of course, he knew the answer, but he didn't know if Cory and Alan would understand. To them, she was their baby sister. To the rest of the world, she was a kickass doctor.

To Finn? She was sexy and bold and fearless and kind. And yes, at times, scary as hell. But only when the situation warranted. In other words, to boil it down, she was quite simply, Erin.

She was Finn's heart. His woman. His lover. Even if her brothers understood—which he doubted—he could never explain.

THE FAMILY GATHERED around a huge dining room table loaded with food. Millie Ashmore presided at one end, her husband Walt at the other. Cory, his wife Tatum, and their two children sat to Walt's left. On the right was Alan. Twice divorced, he arrived with Shelly. A pretty brunette, she was his secretary and girlfriend of two months.

Millie insisted that Finn, the birthday boy, sit next to her with Erin close by on her other side.

"I fixed all your favorites," Millie told Finn as she passed him a bowl filled with a variety of dark, leafy greens—steamed to just the right amount of doneness. "Organic, naturally."

"Jeez, Mom," Alan groused.

"Don't worry," Millie said. "I made lasagna and garlic bread. Though it wouldn't hurt any of us to adopt a few of Finn's healthy habits."

"Finn's been a big influence on my routine," Erin told her mother. "We exercise together almost daily. Multiple times when he feels up to it."

Looking around, Finn was amazed that no caught the way Erin emphasized the word *up*. She practically admitted they were lovers, yet her family seemed oblivious.

Finn shot Erin a look that said, *you will pay*. She merely smiled. Innocent as a newborn lamb.

"Wolves eat little lambs," Finn muttered under his breath. Erin heard every word. Her smile widened as if to say, *bring it on*.

"Everything's delicious," Finn said, turning his attention back to Millie. "You shouldn't have gone to so much trouble."

"What trouble." Millie dismissed his comment with a wave of her hand. "You're family."

"I keep the refrigerator stocked with his health nut food," Erin groused. "Does Finn ever say I made too much of a fuss? Spoiler alert. The answer is never."

"Your housekeeper does the shopping and fills the refrigerator," Finn pointed out as if she didn't know. "The person I should thank is Mrs. Wallander."

When Erin stuck out her tongue a snicker slipped past Finn's lips.

"I forgot how entertaining your verbal sparring can be." Laughing, Millie patted Finn's hand. Her eyes were a shade lighter than Erin's, pale misty rather than sky blue. But just as lively. "We missed you, sweet boy. I know you took me to lunch when you first arrived in town, but tonight makes everything official. Welcome home, sweet Finn."

Finn rarely cried. But Millie's words and open, loving expression almost crumbled his tough guy shell. Ducking his head, he blinked and brought his emotions under control.

Erin never missed anything. When she caught his gaze, she smiled. With a wink, she mouthed one word. *Softy*.

The meal was filled with lively conversation. A few football references slipped under Erin's dictate—she let the moments pass.

Otherwise, they ate, they joked, they laughed. They enjoyed the food and the company.

Next to Erin, Shelly lifted her glass and took a sip of deep, rich chianti. Her dark eyes glittered with mischief as she leaned close.

"The secretaries who I work with think that you and Finn are more than friends," she whispered for Erin's ears only.

Erin wasn't offended by the catty remark. She was annoyed, but in a mild, *the woman's probably harmless*, sort of way.

"Office gossip is the best," Erin nodded, refusing to confirm or deny. Shelly deserved neither response. She thought a mild warning was appropriate. "Don't let Alan hear. He doesn't tolerate employees who spread rumors."

"Gossip? Never!" Shelly blinked her heavily mascaraed lashes as if surprised Erin would suggest such a thing. "Mild speculation."

"I suppose there is a subtle difference." *No, there isn't*, Erin thought. "Depends on the person and the situation."

"Exactly." Shelly beamed at Erin's perceptiveness. "Alan swears nothing is going on. But what do brothers know? Both of mine think I'm still a virgin."

"I'm sure Alan knows exactly what you are."

Erin wondered if Shelly would be wife number three. At least this one smiled. The first two tended to scowl. Often. At everything.

Truthfully, her brother wasn't the best judge of women. He liked a certain type—think Dolly Parton without the wit or intelligence. But in a way, Erin admired a woman like Shelly. Harmless, uncomplicated, and unhindered by a normal person's sense of shame.

"If I lived with someone like Finn Lennox, I'd scale him like *Everest*." Shelly giggled. "Then, I'd conquer him."

A mountain metaphor. Interesting, Erin thought. Maybe Shelly was smarter than she first thought. Her fault. She knew better than to judge a book by its cover.

"Everyone likes Finn." Erin looked across the table and smiled. "Men. Women. Dogs. He draws them in like bees to honey."

"Irresistible." Shelly sighed. "And I love the way he dresses. Like a super-hot fashion model. But with more muscles."

"Not a bad description," Erin laughed, slowly warming to Shelly's brand of charm.

"Not many men can rock a suit in that shade." The stars in Shelly's eyes grew bigger by the second. "What would you call the color?"

"Teal blue." Erin knew for a fact since she helped Finn choose the fabric.

"Turns his eyes a deep silver," Shelly sighed.

"Enough," Alan interrupted. He glared at Erin as though she were responsible for his girlfriend's overtaxed libido.

"Blame Finn, not me," she told her brother as she bit back a smile."

"Hm." Alan huffed. Glancing at Shelly, he handed her a napkin. "Here. Wipe the drool from your chin."

Erin burst out laughing. Alan wasn't happy. Shelly was blissfully unconcerned. Everyone else demanded to know what she found so funny.

"What?" Finn asked when Erin pointed her finger his way.

"You are trouble on a six-foot-three-inch stick," she told him.

"Me?" Finn scoffed. "Why?"

"Simple," she said. "You're just too good looking."

CHAPTER NINETEEN

"I'M TOO GOOD looking?" Finn asked as they left the parking garage and entered the elevator. He pressed the button for the penthouse. "Bad enough to say such a thing in front of your family. Then not to explain? You never fail to amaze."

"Thank you," Erin smiled.

"Not a compliment," he told her.

The doors opened and Finn exited first. Next to Erin, he left behind the bags containing his presents, and the half of a carrot cake her mother pressed on him though she knew he never ate sweets.

"I couldn't explain because of Alan." Erin set the bags near the door. The cake, she brought to the kitchen. She took a plate from the cupboard and turned on the electric kettle. "His girlfriend wouldn't stop gushing about how attractive you are. At some point, I think she compared you to a Greek god."

"So?"

How many men didn't blink when they received such an outrageous compliment and didn't possess an ego the size of the *Empire State Building*? She couldn't believe her best friend, her lover, fell into the small percentile.

"I'm a lucky woman."

One simple sentence, said with complete sincerity, left Finn looking like she poleaxed him.

"What?" Erin asked as she licked a dab of cream cheese frosting from her thumb. "You didn't know?"

Finn touched the ends of her hair and twirled one strand around his finger. He used the connection to gently tug her into his arms

"You never said."

"Does everything need to be put into words?" Erin asked.

When Finn nodded, then nuzzled the spot below her ear that made her entire body sigh with pleasure, her lips curved into a blissful smile.

"As friends, we're solid. Like standing on a hundred feet of bedrock. As lovers, our foundation isn't as secure." Finn laughed. "Poetic, yes?"

"Don't quit your day job," Erin warned. "But I understand what you mean."

"Do you?"

"Until our new relationship matches our old one, nothing should be left unsaid. When you don't communicate, misunderstandings occur. For instance, I want your lips. Here." Erin tilted her head until the curve of her neck was bare and easily accessed. "Are we clear?"

"Crystal."

Finn's mouth found the perfect spot. Erin sighed. When his teeth took a bite, her knees grew weak but the steel band of his arm, firmly anchored around her waist, kept her upright.

"Every garment with more than two buttons should be officially outlawed," he grumbled as he tried to unfasten the tiny row of pearls down her back. "Should I rip the shirt in two?"

"The blouse is vintage *Alexander McQueen*. If you pop a single button, I'll take a pair of scissors to every custom-tailored suit in your closet," Erin warned, knowing how to hit Finn below the belt without raising a finger.

"Ouch." Finn sighed. "What to do?"

Reaching back, Erin unfastened the first five pearls. Giving him a warning look, she raised her hands over her head.

"Up and over," she instructed. "Carefully."

Known as the wide receiver with the softest hands in the league, Finn used his skill to remove Erin's blouse without incident. Reverently, he lay the garment over the arm of the sofa.

"Nothing better than a man who appreciates fashion. Now, where were we?" she asked as she loosened his tie and slid the length of silk from around his neck.

Before Finn could remind her, the intercom connected to the lobby buzzed. They groaned in unison.

"Don't answer," Finn demanded. "Nothing good can come when you get a call from the desk in the middle of the night."

"Eight-thirty isn't late." Erin glanced from her bra to the video screen, to her blouse.

"No. Please," Finn pleaded, shaking his head. "Don't make me undress you again. I'll go."

"If you insist." Wearing nothing above the waist but a few pieces of strategically assembled lace, Erin was happy to oblige.

"You. Over there." Finn pointed toward the bank of windows. "Stay completely out of camera range. Understood?"

"Because I don't get off on exhibitionism, I will follow your bossy dictates." Erin waggled a warning finger in front of Finn's face. "This time."

"Jesus," Finn muttered as he crossed the room. "The woman doesn't give an inch without taking three."

"I heard that," she called out.

"You were meant to."

Hiding a smile, Finn pushed the button that connected him to the lobby's front desk. The familiar face of the night manager filled the screen. Always calm and collected, for once, she seemed a bit out of sorts.

"Mr. Lennox." Anne Cranston sighed with relief. "Thank goodness you answered."

"Is something wrong?"

"A man is at the front desk." Visibly uncomfortable, Anne cleared her throat. "He claims to be your father."

"Claims my ass."

Finn closed his eyes when he recognized Jerry Lennox's slurred voice. He could practically smell the alcohol from here.

"Look at the eyes, missy." Jerry shouted each word. Anne winced. "Gray. Just like my boy's."

"He's harmless," Finn assured Anne. At least he used to be. Now, his father was a wild card. "Don't worry. I'll be right down."

Taking a shuddering breath into his lungs, Finn rubbed his eyes. It didn't matter how often he faced his father's crap; he was never prepared for the next level of awful.

Erin wrapped her arms around his waist from behind. Her cheek against his back, just knowing she cared, that she would be here when he returned, gave him a much-needed boost.

"I have to go to him."

"I know," she nodded, then exhaled. "Bring him up."

"You don't want him here," Finn told her. "I don't want him anywhere near you."

"The lobby is out of the question and you don't know what he'll do if you take him to a public place," Erin reasoned. "Your father needs to sober up. Unfortunately, you're the only person he has who will help."

"Erin—"

"I can stay in my office. He'll never know I'm here—unless he needs medical attention. Don't hesitate to call if something happens." Erin pushed Finn into the elevator. She handed him a plastic garbage bag and shrugged. "Just in case."

You think of everything," Finn said as he tucked the bag into his pocket.

"I worked a six-month rotation in the ER when I was a resident," she explained. "There isn't much I haven't seen."

"Are you sure about this?" Worried, Finn met her steady gaze. "I can just take him to a hotel until he dries out."

"And get your picture plastered all over the internet." Erin shook her head. "The apartment is a controlled atmosphere. You can talk.

Or yell. Or cry. The walls are thick. I won't hear a thing. Neither will anyone else."

"I won't cry," Finn said.

"*He* might."

Giving his hand one last encouraging squeeze, Erin backed out and let the heavy metal doors shut behind her. Before he had time to think further than the need to brace himself for whatever his father had in mind, he stepped into the lobby.

"Mr. Lennox." Anne Cranston rushed to his side. Dressed in a simple white blouse, black pencil skirt, and matching pumps, the tap of her heels was muffled by the thick carpet. "Please forgive me. Your father wouldn't leave and he's inebriated. I was about to call the police when he mentioned your name."

"You did the right thing," Finn assured her. "Jerry is my responsibility."

Anne nodded.

"I plan to make him understand that this building is off-limits," Finn said. "However, if my father ever returns and I'm not here? Follow through on your first instinct. Call the police."

Sprawled on a black sofa located in the reception area, Jerry Lennox's eyes were closed. Not sure if he was passed out or simply resting, Finn shook his father's arm.

"Dad?" Finn shook him again. "Dad!"

"Took you long enough."

Jerry hiccupped between each word. The smell of stale liquor, bad breath, the faint overtone of body odor, and something else wafted from his father's limp form. Urine? Finn winced.

He tried to get Jerry onto his feet.

More rag doll than human, the job of keeping his father in an upright position proved impossible. Finn finally gave up and hefted Jerry over his shoulder.

Anne held the elevator doors until Finn was inside. He nodded his thanks.

"When did you start drinking?"

"Mm." Jerry gagged. "Two days ago? Maybe."

Finn meant in general, but he didn't bother to correct the mistake. When his father made a heaving sound, he quickly fished the bag from his pocket.

"If you need to throw up, use this," Finn instructed. "If you toss your cookies on me, I'll drop you on your bony ass, old man. Understand."

A second later, Jerry heaved his guts—mostly into the bag. Finn reminded himself to thank Erin. Profusely. On his knees.

When they reached the apartment, Finn looked around for a safe place that his father couldn't ruin with another bout of sickness or the stench of his clothes. Again, Erin saved the day.

While Finn was gone, she rolled up the antique rug that normally covered the center of the hardwood floors and covered the sofa and surrounding floor.

Where the hell did she find an industrial-sized sheet of plastic at this time of night? Finn wondered as he lay his father onto his side.

Taking the bag full of puke, Finn gingerly carried it across the room and into the garbage can. First thing in the morning he would throw out the trash—along with his father.

Along with the plastic-lined sofa, Erin left half a dozen bottles of electrolyte infused sports drinks, water, and several packets of wet wipes were lined up like good little soldiers on a nearby table and a note.

Force plenty of fluids. Erin wrote. *The more you get into him, the faster the alcohol will pass through his bloodstream. Not a miracle cure, but better than nothing. The wet wipes are self-explanatory.*

Opening a packet, Finn lifted his father into a sitting position. Once he cleaned away the drying vomit to the best of his ability, he held a sports drink to Jerry's mouth.

"Want whiskey."

"You can't have everything." Finn should know. He wished for the father he once knew. Instead, a gambling-addicted drunk showed up on his doorstep.

Sometimes life was a lead-plated motherfucker.

Finn grabbed two pair of his sweatpants and a couple of fleece pullovers from the downstairs laundry room and found a pair of sneakers next to the dryer. He changed out of his suit and put the other things aside for when his father was sober enough to take a shower.

Soon as possible, he planned to find the nearest blast furnace and incinerate every dirty, smelly, sweat-caked item—right down to the underwear and crusty tennis shoes.

For the next hour, Finn alternated between pouring water, juice, and energy drinks down Jerry's throat and praying the liquids wouldn't come back up. By hour number two, his prayers were answered.

Less drunk but not quite sober, Jerry finally passed out. Or into a deep slumber. Finn didn't know enough about his father's sleeping habits to tell the difference.

Deciding he was safe to leave Jerry alone for a few minutes, Finn padded down the hall to Erin's office. Quietly as possible, he opened the door.

"No need to tiptoe," she said, looking up from a pile of papers. "I'm awake."

"You should have gone to bed." Finn sank to the floor at her feet. "Jerry wouldn't have noticed."

"How can I sleep when you might need me?"

"I always need you. But not tonight. Don't touch me," he warned when Erin reached out. "Between the puking and the rest of the foreign substances lurking on Jerry's clothes—don't ask, don't tell—I reek. Though by the time I'm done, my olfactory nerves will be permanently shot."

"Do you want a medical fact about your sense of smell? Or should I forget I'm a doctor and just shift directly into girlfriend mode?"

"I'm afraid your fun medical facts would be wasted on me." Finn sighed. "Too tired."

"Girlfriend mode it is."

Ignoring his warning, Erin placed her palms on Finn's face, kissed him lightly, then placed his head on her lap. When she surreptitiously fanned the air, he found just enough energy to smile.

"Told you."

Erin took a match from her desk, struck the tip, and lit the scented candle she kept on her desk. The smell of vanilla/cranberry warred with the odor wafting from Finn. For the time being, Finn won.

"What did your father do to create such a god-awful stench," Erin asked, sliding the candle as close as possible.

"The better question would be what didn't he do?" Wrapping his arms around her legs, Finn allowed himself a moment to relax. "Between the vomiting and the belching and…"

"And?" Erin prompted.

"I don't even want to know what's going on in his pants." Finn opened one eye. "You're not even phased by what I told you?"

"A homeless man came into the ER with live maggots on his body." Erin smoothed back Finn's hair. "Better you don't know where we found them."

"I'm too tired to care." Though he wanted to stay, Finn forced himself to stand.

"Poor baby."

When Erin tried to hug him, Finn drew the line.

"Later. After I shower seven or eight times." He stretched his arms over his head. "Thank God for the bye week. If I had to report for practice in the morning, I wouldn't be able to tell a flea-flicker from a forward pass."

"During a flea-flicker, you get the pass then lateral to a teammate." Erin laughed when Finn's mouth fell open. "My best friend is a wide receiver. I may not like the game but it seemed only logical that I should understand the rules and regulations."

"Damn, your brain is sexy." Finn pulled Erin in for a brief but scorching hot kiss that left them both gasping for air. "Sorry. Couldn't resist."

"Anytime," Erin assured him. "Your outside might stink to high heaven, but your breath is minty fresh."

"I probably have time for another round."

Finn reached for Erin, only to have his hand swatted away.

"Go check on your father. Make him take a shower." Erin tapped her fingers on the desk. "As for my sofa? Even with the plastic…"

"Needs fumigating?" Finn nodded. He understood.

"Or we could replace everything and start fresh." Erin shrugged. "Overkill, I know, but there's such a thing as phantom odors. If you think something smells, it does."

"First, let me get Jerry on his feet and out the door. We'll talk a total remodel later."

As Finn left the office, he found himself laughing. Felt good. All thanks to Erin. She had a way of pulling him out of the doldrums when nothing else could.

"You're back." Jerry sat on the sofa, head in his hands. "Thought maybe you skipped out."

"I live here." Finn grabbed the clothes and sneakers from the table. "Long as you're awake, let's get you cleaned up. After, while you shower, I'll heat up some soup."

"Finn—"

"Whatever you have to say can wait." Finn pointed toward the open bathroom door. "I put out some fresh towels. Everything else you need is in the cabinet above the sink including a toothbrush and mouth wash. Please use both."

Finn waited until the door closed before rushing up the stairs to his room. He dumped his clothes, jumped in the shower, and was back downstairs in less than ten minutes.

As Finn stirred a saucepan of tomato bisque with one hand and toweled his hair dry with the other, he almost felt human again. Jerry shuffled in just as he poured the soup into a bowl.

"Sit." Finn nodded to the counter where he set out a spoon and napkin. "Would you like a cup of hot tea?"

"Maybe later." Jerry swirled the spoon around the bowl, staring at the contents but not eating. "I need money."

The brash request wasn't a surprise. Finn gave his father points for coming right to the point once he was sober enough to string together a full sentence.

But for the first time since Finn had a sizable amount of money in the bank, his father was out of luck. The buck, literally, stopped here.

"No." Finn leaned his hip against the counter and crossed his arms. "You won't get another penny from me."

"You should have stayed in Chicago," Jerry said. "Or signed with Denver. Or Minnesota. Any place but Seattle."

"What the hell are you talking about?" Finn scoffed. "I grew up watching the Knights. You took me to a game for my ninth birthday. Playing for Seattle is a dream come true."

"I said a prayer of thanks when you were drafted by the Bears." Jerry rubbed his temples, a sneer curling his upper lip. "Finally got you away from that bitch."

"Back up, old man," Finn warned, his voice vibrating with anger. "You're about to cross a line you can't come back from."

Desperate, watching as his source of endless money slipped away before his eyes, Jerry ignored Finn's warning.

"I tried to keep you away from her, but you wouldn't listen." His father smashed his fist onto the counter. "She sucked you in, made you think you were her friend. Did she wait until you turned eighteen, or did she fuck you right away?"

Finn's hands curled into fists. He closed his eyes and counted to ten. When his lids opened, the haze was still there, but the urge to throw Jerry across the room was under control.

"Get out. Now."

"Can't you see how much better off you were in Chicago? Away from her influence?" Jerry whined. "Look what happened the second you came back. She convinced you to toss your old man aside like yesterday's trash."

"Erin had nothing to do with my decision." Finn felt an odd calm settle over him. "You're the reason. Stop blaming her for your mistakes."

Jerry's shoulders slumped and for a minute, he thought his father might admit defeat. He should have known the old man had one last card to play.

"What if I go to the commissioner of the national football league and tell him I placed bets on dozens of your games." Jerry's smile turned nasty. "Won't they be surprised to discover their fresh-faced poster boy shaved points to help his old man make money?"

After years of sinking lower and lower, his father achieved the impossible. He managed to burrow twenty feet below rock bottom. And Finn was fine with letting him keep on digging.

"Where's your proof," he asked. "The commissioner will listen, but he won't act unless you can prove your allegations."

"You're right. You didn't do anything wrong. Why would I have proof? Then again, facts don't always matter. Not these days."

Jerry was on a roll, enamored with the sound of his own voice. He couldn't see that Finn wasn't fazed by his threats. Or he simply didn't care.

"All I need to tank your reputation are a few strategically placed lies and innuendos." Jerry laughed. "The rest I'll leave to your adoring public. *Maybe* the league will let you keep playing. But the sweet endorsement deals and endless perks will dry up faster than you can say Grand Jury inditement."

Finn had to laugh. He sure as hell wasn't going to cry. Jerry watched in amazement.

"Look," he said, determined to go down swinging. "If you pay me off. I'll keep my mouth shut."

"How much?" For some perverse reason, Finn wanted to know.

"Five million?" Jerry shrugged. "Seems like a reasonable amount all things considered."

"Here's my deal," Finn said. "If you leave now. I won't have you arrested for extortion."

"What?" Jerry's eyes darted around the kitchen as though he expected the police to jump out from behind the refrigerator.

"Clock's ticking." Finn tapped the counter, counting off the seconds. "You have thirty seconds to move your ass out of here."

"You'll be sorry." Jerry tripped over his feet and stumbled from the room. "Mark my words."

The elevator opened, then closed, with ten seconds to spare.

Finn's head fell forward. He didn't know how he felt. Angry? Sure. But he was too tired to work up a lot of steam. Sad? Maybe. A little. Jerry would always be his father and he hoped with time the good memories from his childhood were what he remembered first.

Mostly, Finn felt relief. Not for Jerry, but because Erin didn't witness the last ugly exchange between father and son.

"I'm thankful she couldn't hear what Jerry said about her."

"Sorry."

Finn's head whipped around. Erin stood in the hall, not five feet away. With a sheepish smile, she shrugged.

"I guess the walls aren't as thick as I thought."

CHAPTER TWENTY

FINN CLOSED HIS eyes, peeked to make certain Erin wasn't an exhaustion induced hallucination and groaned. He always considered himself to be a lucky man. He worked hard, didn't cut corners, played the game the right way.

However, anyone who ever stepped onto a football field could tell you that making it from high school, through college, and to the NFL took more than talent and determination. You also needed good fortune.

Call it what you wanted. An angel on your shoulder. Karma. Or plain old-fashioned luck. Either way, through lack of opportunity or injury, or personal demons, most people never reached the heights of playing professional football.

A long career was a rarity. Just over three years was the average. Finn survived a decade. A strong body and mind helped. But luck had to be on his side.

Tonight, between Jerry's threats and Erin's untimely entrance, he had to wonder if his run of good fortune had come to an end.

"How much did you hear?" Finn asked.

Erin found the spot opposite him and hoisted herself onto the counter. The extra height put her eyes even with his.

Finn winced.

"Don't beat yourself up. I learned long ago how your father feels about me. Tonight was hardly the first time he called me a bitch or something more colorful. Cradle robber comes to mind." Erin chuckled. "Though I think blood-sucking harpy is my favorite."

"Stop." Shaking his head, Finn groaned. "How can you laugh? Unless you want me to put a fist through the wall, just stop."

"I'm sorry." Erin sighed. "Would you rather see me cry?"

"No." Finn walked into her arms and held tight. "God no."

"Good." Erin kissed his temple. "Jerry Lennox isn't worth a single one of my tears. Or yours."

"I didn't cry," Finn told her.

"Yes, you did." Erin tapped his chest. "In here."

"I weep on the inside?" Finn scoffed, then sighed. "Maybe you're right. I don't know."

"You're allowed to be sad. If you want to hit the wall, be my guest. It's only plaster and paint." Taking his hand, she ran her thumb over each knuckle. "If you break a bone, will you miss any games?"

Finn shook his head. Erin never changed. Hopefully, she never would.

"You smiled." She tapped his bottom lip. "Almost laughed and the world didn't implode simply because you forgot to be sad—just for a second."

"Let's go to bed."

"Should we?" Erin asked.

"Mm,' he nodded. "Hold tight."

Placing her legs around him, Finn tightened his grip on Erin's waist, stood up straight, headed toward the stairs.

"I can walk," she said.

"I like you where you are."

"Okay." With a contented sigh, Erin rested her head on his shoulder. "You do all the work. I'll just enjoy the ride."

"Why can't you always be this accommodating?" Finn asked as he pushed open the door to her bedroom. "My life would be so much simpler."

"Bull-swoggle," Erin scoffed. "You'd be bored silly if I rolled over and played the simpering miss."

"True." Finn lay her on the bed. Too tired to undress, he flopped down beside her. "But just for tonight, a little simpering isn't a bad thing."

"Just for tonight," Erin agreed. She arranged the covers over them and took his hand in hers.

"Is swoggle even a word?" Finn asked after a few seconds ticked by.

"Absolutely. Look it up. I dare you." Erin snickered. "You'll be surprised."

"Tomorrow." Finn closed his eyes. He wasn't close to falling asleep, but with Erin close, he could finally start to relax. "Remind me."

"I will." Erin turned onto her side. She placed her hand on his chest. "Finn?"

"Hm?"

"About what your father said." A worried tone entered her voice. "What if he follows through on his threat and reports you to the commissioner of the NFL?"

"What?" Finn cracked one eyelid. "Do you think I'm guilty?"

Erin punched him.

"Ouch." Rubbing his arm, Finn frowned. Erin might look like a delicate flower, but she had freaking fists of steel.

"You don't cheat," she said. Full stop. End of story. "But even if Jerry has no proof, he could cause trouble. One thing he's right about. These days, the truth is whatever people want to believe."

Erin looked so earnest Finn had to smile.

"Did I say something funny?" Erin asked. "I don't think so."

"I love how worried you are about me." Finn raised her hand to his lips. "You can relax. Jerry's threats are a non-starter."

"How can you be certain?" Erin's gaze narrowed. "You know something. Tell me."

"The NFL head office already knows about Jerry," Finn explained. "Before I signed my rookie contract with Chicago, my agent and I, along with legal counsel, met with the commissioner. I explained that my father is a gambler and that he might bet on my games. He did when I was in college."

"You never said." Erin let out a long, sad sigh. "Even before you earned a salary, Jerry made money off your talent. I'm sorry."

"He didn't make much." Finn shrugged. "Jerry always lost more than he won."

"But UW won a lot of games when you played." Erin's eyes widened. "You mean he bet against you? Your father?"

"As I said, Jerry's a lousy gambler. Which worked out for me," Finn told her. "Since Dad didn't get rich, or break even, the commissioner decided to overlook my unfortunate family connection."

"Smart man." Erin grinned. "And smart Finny. You put all your father's sins on the table before he could use them against you. And they say you're just a pretty face."

"Who says?" Finn asked with a half-smile. "Name names."

"I'll make a list," Erin laughed. "You were proactive, and everything worked out. The good guys won."

"I didn't get off scot-free." Finn shook his head when a spark of worry flared in Erin's blue eyes. "Nothing terrible. I was on a type of probation for the first five years I played."

"Probation?" Erin was outraged. "Why slap you down when you didn't do anything?"

"The NFL is a multi-billion-dollar business. They don't work on sentimentality or goodwill. A big reason the league has lasted when others failed is that they think of the bottom dollar first. Second, they always cover their ass before anyone else's."

"Yours included." Erin sighed. "But it's such a nice ass."

"Compliment accepted," Finn said. "I don't blame the commissioner for his decision to monitor my games with a fine-tooth comb. Any irregularities on my part and I was gone. Tossed out of the game for the rest of my life. I agreed not to contest the decision."

"Harsh," Erin huffed. "I don't suppose you had any choice."

"Not if I wanted to play," Finn nodded. "The ruling turned out to be good for the NFL, and me. They were covered from any wrongdoing and when my probation ended, the commission trusted my word. Plus, my reputation was solid."

"Five years in, you were a superstar." Erin nodded, understanding how the world worked. "A squeaky-clean golden boy. Your commissioner must have been on cloud nine."

"Be fair," Finn said. "He took a chance on me."

"Please," Erin snorted. "If something had gone wrong, the only person required to pay a price was you."

Finn wasn't naïve. The NFL was a cutthroat business. But the lifestyle he enjoyed wouldn't be possible without football. No organization was perfect. Lucky for him, the good far outweighed the bad.

"Any more questions?" Finn asked. He yawned. "Finally, I think I can fall asleep."

"Your mind is clear." Erin brushed his hair back from his face. "Because you talked things through with me. I'm your sounding board. If you don't want your brain to clog, you need to tell me everything."

"Drives you crazy to think there might be a little corner of my life that you haven't infiltrated." Finn shook his head. "A few secrets, even between best friends, aren't a bad thing."

"You have secrets?" Erin shot to a sitting position. "Something not related to football?"

"Good night, Erin."

"Tell me." She shook his arm. "Come on. You know you want to."

Erin knew how he felt about her. And he told her about the deal he made with the NFL before his rookie season. Finn had nothing left. Where she was concerned, he was an open book.

However, a little mystery never hurt—even if it was all in Erin's mind.

"Sleep. Please," he mumbled.

"Fine. Whatever."

Amused, Finn reached to pull her close only to find the bed beside him empty.

"Where are you going?" he asked when he caught Erin leaving the room. "Did the hospital call? No. I didn't hear your phone ring."

"You need sleep? I need water." She gave him a reassuring smile. "Relax. I'll be right back."

"If I don't have you in my arms in five minutes, I'll come and get you," he told her.

"You'll be in dreamland before I get back." Erin gave him a quick kiss. When he tried to grab her hand, she deftly avoided capture. "Don't start something you can't finish."

"I have enough left in the tank for some fun and games." Finn stifled another yawn. "Maybe."

"Live to make love another day." Erin winked. "I'll remind you where we left off."

Finn closed his eyes, a smile on his lips. Before the door clicked shut, he was asleep.

CHAPTER TWENTY-ONE

ERIN GRABBED TWO bottles from the refrigerator. She didn't expect Finn to be awake when she returned, but better safe than sorry. He might be thirsty. If he was, she didn't feel like sharing.

Stopping at the bottom of the steps, Erin unscrewed the cap and took a deep, satisfying drink. She raised the bottle again, then froze, certain she heard a strange noise.

The alarm was set—she made certain before she left her office.

There it was again. Like something scraping against the wall. Frowning, Erin concentrated, trying to pinpoint the location.

Finn's room? Did he leave her bed and go in search of something? But what would he need that couldn't wait until morning?

Erin peered into the darkness. Familiar with the layout of her apartment, she hadn't bothered to turn on any lights. The glow of the moon through the windows was enough for her to see by. But something told her she wasn't alone.

Heart pounding, Erin tapped the screen on her phone and pressed 911 into the keypad. With her thumb hovering over the call button, she reached over and flipped on the lights.

The distinct sound of a human gasp drew Erin's eyes up the stairs. A few feet from the door to Finn's room, she found Jerry Lennox. Hair standing in every direction, eyes wide with surprise, he had a bag slung over one shoulder like a certain jolly old soul who visited good little girls and boys.

But Jerry wasn't Santa Clause and tonight wasn't Christmas Eve.

Eve didn't need to ask what was in the bag. Finn liked expensive things. The collection of Rolex watches tucked neatly in individual cubbies was worth a small fortune. Gold cuff links. The platinum ring Erin gave him as a gift. A man desperate for money wouldn't need to look far.

Jerry was a thief. A bastard who didn't hesitate to steal from his own son. Erin couldn't say she was surprised.

"Trapped like the rat you are."

"You've been a thorn in my side since the day I let you into my house." Jerry sneered. "Babysitter? More like a predator. You have him convinced that you changed his life. Bullshit. My boy didn't stand a chance."

"If Finn never met me, he would have been fine." Erin had no doubt. "But he needed a friend. And that's all I was. Sweet. Innocent."

"Right," Jerry scoffed. Keeping his eyes on Erin, he started down the stairs. "You were never innocent."

"Yes, I was. You're the one with the dirty mind." Erin shook her head, unable to understand him. Certain she never would.

"You took him from me." Jerry stumbled to the landing and fell to his knees. When he looked up, he sniffled as though about to cry. "Let me go and we'll call it even."

"Save the crocodile tears." Erin put her phone to her ear. "Hello? Yes. Send help. There's an intruder in my home."

Holding Jerry's gaze, Erin rattled off her address.

"Yes," she said. "I'll stay on the line."

"You fucking bitch," Jerry screamed.

"Dad!" From above them, Finn gripped the banister. "What are you doing?"

Jerry didn't answer. Jumping to his feet, he swung the bag at Erin. She avoided contact but lost her footing and fell. On the way down, her cheek hit the arm of a chair.

Finn rushed down the stairs. Desperate, he pulled Erin into his arms.

"Are you hurt?" He touched the cut on her cheek. "I'll kill the bastard."

"And go to prison? Not while I have a breath left in my body." Erin winced. "The police will be here any second. Let them do their job."

"What if he gets away?"

Finn tried to rise, but Erin stopped him.

"The elevator's locked down," she told him. "Jerry isn't going anywhere except to jail."

CHAPTER TWENTY-TWO

ERIN REFUSED TO go to the hospital. She was a doctor, she reminded Finn.

"A doctor who treats herself has a fool for a patient," he told her.

"Lawyer, not doctor," Erin said." I doubt Abraham Lincoln would appreciate you bastardizing his quote."

"Same difference." Finn hovered in the door of the bathroom as Erin placed a bandage over the antiseptic she applied to her cheek. "I have a small cut. Nothing's broken."

"No thanks to me," he muttered.

Needing his touch, Erin put her arms around Finn's waist. A second later, he hugged her back. *Better*, she thought. *Much better.*

"Blame your father. I do."

"If I'd cut him off years ago, tonight wouldn't have happened." A shudder ran through Finn's body. "Jerry was desperate. When I think about what might have happened."

"You know how I feel about what-ifs." Erin shook her head. "I'm fine. In a few days, you won't know anything happened. Jerry, on the other hand, won't be as lucky. When my cut is healed, he'll still be in jail."

"I can't believe he hid in the hall closet." Finn rubbed a hand over his face. "I should have escorted him out of the building. Kicked his sorry ass to the curb."

"Then he would still be out there. Causing trouble," Erin reminded him. "Don't get me wrong. I didn't enjoy the burglary or attempted assault."

"Jesus." Again, Finn's strong, solid frame shook with a shuddering sigh.

"However," Erin continued. "The results are what matter. Tomorrow afternoon, we'll give our statements to the police. Charges will be pressed."

"A man shouldn't be happy to see his father behind bars."

"I'd be disappointed if you were." Erin curled her fingers into the front of Finn's shirt. Tipping her head, she met his troubled gaze. "At least you can stop worrying. No one will hound him for money. He'll get three regular meals a day. A place to sleep. A regular shower. And no alcohol."

"For how long?" Finn tucked a strand of hair behind Erin's ear and sighed. "My guess is, not long enough."

"The length of Jerry's sentence will be up to the prosecutor and the judge." Erin rubbed her cheek against Finn's hand. "Help with his addiction will be available. The rest is up to him."

Finn tucked Erin into bed before joining her.

"I have a question," he said, taking her in his arms.

"I'll give you an answer," she promised. "If I can."

"The cop in the fancy suit. The one who couldn't stop smiling at you? Who is he?"

Erin wanted to laugh at Finn's description. For a man who owned his share of *fancy suits*, the sneer in his voice was a tad ironic.

"Lieutenant Bronson. Malachi."

"You're on a first-name basis?" Finn didn't sound pleased. "And why would a detective, a lieutenant, show up for a burglary?"

"He was passing by, saw the police car, and stopped because he knew I live in the building." Erin shrugged. "No big deal."

"Why does he know where you live?" Finn demanded. "Did you date him?"

Jealous Finnegan was adorable, Erin thought, hiding her smile in the crook of his arm.

"We met a while back when he was in charge of a stalking case involving Darcy Stratham."

"The Knights' general manager?" Finn frowned. "Was she okay?"

"Malachi caught the person. He's good at his job," Erin said. "Because he and Darcy stayed friendly after the case closed, I invited him to a party at my apartment last Christmas."

"And that's why he knows where you live." Finn nodded. "I still don't like his face."

"Are you worried I might think Malachi is prettier than you?" Erin shook her head. "Impossible. I only have eyes for you."

"Right." Finn knew better, but since he trusted Erin to look, not touch, he didn't push the point.

"I can't believe it's only three in the morning." Sleep calling, Erin closed her eyes. "Feels like my body aged ten years."

"You're stiff from the fall." Finn gently massaged her shoulders.

"So good," Erin sighed. "Don't stop."

"Sleep," Finn told her as his magic fingers continued to pull the soreness from her muscles.

"You, too."

Sensing Finn's affirmative nod, Erin drifted off. She didn't dream. The next time she opened her eyes, she was surprised to see by the clock that she only slept for an hour.

For a second, her mind fuzzy, Erin couldn't figure out what woke her. She stretched, her hand landing on nothing but a quilt, sheets, and the mattress. No Finn. She frowned. Odd how quickly she'd grown used to having him in her bed. Without him, she felt unsettled and restless.

Finn couldn't have gone far. If Erin waited, he'd be back. But something didn't feel right. A niggling feeling at the base of her skull told her he needed her. If she was wrong, the only thing she wasted was a few steps. If she was right? She couldn't say.

All Erin knew was that she had to find Finn.

Pulling on a robe, Erin padded barefoot along the hallway. From the corner of her eye, she noticed a light in the kitchen, but no Finn. Frowning, she jogged down the stairs.

The light came from just above the stovetop. Erin could think of no logical reason for anyone to turn the thing on. Not in the wee hours of the morning.

Rounding the corner of the granite-topped island, Erin reached to turn off the light and froze as her foot landed on a half-empty box of *Ding Dongs*. Like a surreal trail of breadcrumbs, her gaze landed on a bag of *Doritos* followed by a wrapper from a giant-size bar of *Hershey's* chocolate.

Half a dozen stray *Gummy Bears*, their little bodies strewn in every direction as though victims of a teeny, tiny hit and run, led Erin around the island's corner. What she found made her gasp.

"Finn?"

Smiling, eyes glazed over, his mouth circled with chocolate and tortilla chip crumbs, Finn held a gallon of *Coffee Crunch* ice cream in one hand, a bottle of *Michelob* in the other.

Horrified, Erin watched as Finn poured beer into the carton. Scooping out a spoonful, he raised the dripping, melting concoction to his mouth, slid it into his mouth, swallowed, then sighed.

"What are you doing?" Erin asked, wondering if she was still in bed, deep in a ghoulish nightmare.

"Erin!" Finn let out a demented laugh. He held out the ice cream carton. "Want a bite?"

Erin shook her head. Dressed in nothing but a pair of low-riding purple and red board shorts, the man possessed the same gray eyes and auburn hair as her Finn. The long athlete's legs seemed familiar, as did the trim hips and washboard flat stomach. The strong shoulders tapered to a pair of muscular arms that she would have sworn not long ago held her close while she slept.

Physically, he looked like the man Erin knew. But her Finn who shunned anything processed or prepackaged, would not have gone within a mile of so many empty calories.

Erin didn't know what was wrong, but in the morning, he would hate himself.

"Most people put chocolate sauce on ice cream. Why beer?"

Erin asked the first question that popped into her head. Why put beer on ice cream was hardly the point, all the things considered. But nothing about Finn's behavior was close to normal. She was at a loss about what to say or do.

If Erin's question was odd, Finn's answer beat hers by a mile on the weirdness scale.

"Ran out of wine."

Holy vomit inducer. Finn mixed wine, beer, and ice cream. Erin hadn't consumed a single bite and her stomach felt queasy.

Joining Finn on the floor, Erin crossed her legs and tried to reason with him. Which wouldn't be easy. He was drunk and on a sugar high. She couldn't say for sure since her experience equaled zero, but the two seemed like a bad combination.

"Finn. You don't like ice cream," she reminded him.

"Love ice cream." He snorted. "Can't eat it or I'll get fat."

"Then why don't you stop?"

"Started with cake. Yum," Finn sighed. "So good."

"You ate what was left of your birthday cake?" Erin groaned. "Your body isn't used to so much fat and sugar. Your stomach won't tolerate much more."

The lobby intercom buzzed.

"Pizza's here!" Finn declared.

"You didn't." When he nodded, Erin sighed and rolled to her feet. "Unbelievable. When the man falls off the wagon, he falls hard."

Erin paid for the delivery. Three large pizzas with everything but the kitchen sink on top. She left the boxes by the elevator. In the

174

kitchen, she found Finn slumped against the dishwasher. The carton lay on the floor, ice cream and beer forming a pool of goo.

"Oh, Finny." Erin knelt beside him. "You are going to be so sick in the morning."

Finn gaged, twice. His hand covered his mouth as he tried and failed to scramble to his feet. Erin knew they had no time. Instead of the bathroom, she dragged him to the sink and held his head as everything he put into his body, came back up in a multicolored gush.

Again, and again, Finn's stomach rebelled. Medically, Erin understood that the only thing he threw up was food and alcohol. But at some point, she swore she saw something vital. Like a kidney. Or a large chunk of his intestine.

"I'm dying," Finn proclaimed in a voice that barely reached above a whisper.

Erin held back a laugh as she supported most of his weight up the flight of stairs. Finn was such a strong, vital man. To witness his temporary downfall was distressing and kind of hilarious. He would recover. Thank goodness. But until then, her mighty hero was weak as the proverbial baby. And just as helpless.

After giving him a sponge bath—neither of them would have survived a shower without a head injury—Erin maneuvered Finn into bed. She placed a hand on his forehead, relieved to find the skin clammy, but cool.

"Sleep it off, big boy."

Finn groaned but didn't open his eyes. Erin gave him one last look before she girded her loins and headed back to the kitchen to clean up the mess. Just the thought made her nauseous. But sometimes in a relationship, you had to do what you had to do.

One thing was certain. Finn owed her. Big time. A fact she wasn't likely to let him forget.

CHAPTER TWENTY-THREE

FINN OPENED HIS eyes. For a moment, his mind was blissfully blank. Not for long. He didn't remember everything, but enough memories remained to make him wish the floor would open and suck him in before he had to face the day. Or Erin. Especially Erin.

"Hello, sunshine."

Nope. He wasn't ready.

"You can't run. Not the way your head must feel. And you can't hide." Erin pulled the covers from his head. "Sit up. I brought water, hot tea, and a pain reliever."

"Erin…"

"I know," she sighed. "You only take holistic medicine. But the way you abused your precious body, a couple of over-the-counter tablets won't kill you."

Finn scrubbed a hand over his face. Between the day's growth of stubble and the sleep he needed to wash from his eyes, he wanted to stay as far away from his reflection as possible.

"You look nice," he said, taking in her silky blonde hair, crisp white blouse, and fashionably faded blue jeans. Without makeup, fresh-faced and rested, she could have passed for twenty.

"You look like something even the cat wouldn't want to drag in." With a sympathetic smile, Finn wasn't sure he deserved, Erin handed him the water. "Drink up. You'll feel better."

Taking pain killers—with his head pounding like a jackhammer on steroids, he wasn't about to argue—Finn emptied the water in one breath. He wrapped his hands around the cup of hot tea as he gathered his thoughts and words.

"About last night."

"You put on quite a show," she said.

"Did I?" Finn cleared his throat. "I suppose you want an explanation."

Erin sat on the edge of the bed. She seemed more amused than angry. Always a good sign.

"Wouldn't you want to know what happened? More to the point, why?" She shook her head. "I've seen alcoholics go off the wagon but never a health nut."

"I'm sorry."

"You're allowed." Erin laughed. "Not to that extent—for your sweet body's sake. Perhaps you should enjoy a sliver of cheesecake or a couple of *Peppermint Patties*. Then you won't be tempted to eat twenty-years of goodies in one sitting."

"I'm sorry my father hurt you." Finn touched Erin's cheek, his guts twisting when he noticed the bruise spreading out from under the bandage. "I'm sorry I let him."

"You consumed half the contents of the refrigerator and heaved your guts because of a cut on my cheek? Finn." Erin took his hand. Kissing the palm, she sighed. "I'm sorry."

"Don't you dare apologize."

"I need to," she insisted. "I forget that just because you look like *Superman*, you're as human as the rest of us."

"You don't want to kick me out?" Finn tried to keep the need, the fear from his voice. Erin saw right through him.

"And throw away twenty years of training," she teased. "Until last night, I thought you were practically perfect. What a relief to discover you have a few flaws. Takes the pressure off me."

"I'd kiss you, but…"

"Brush first." Laughing, Erin made a face. Then, she kissed his cheek. His forehead. The end of his nose. Finally, his lips. "Not bad."

"I'll do better. Give me fifteen minutes." Finn stood, swayed, and fell back onto the bed. "Maybe twenty would be better."

"Take your time." Erin pulled him to his feet and walked him to the bathroom. "I'm not going anywhere."

Finn tugged on his ear, afraid to ask. But he had to know.

"Did I say anything weird?" He shrugged. "I have a feeling I did. But I can't remember."

"Hm." Erin considered his question. "No. Unless you mean when you said I love you, Erin."

"I did? When?"

"When your head was in the sink," Erin told him. "Between upchucks."

"No." Finn's head dropped to his chest. He quickly walked into the bathroom and shut the door. "No. No. No!"

"You don't love me?" she asked, not letting him off the hook. "Despite the situation, you sounded sincere."

"Of course, I love you," Finn yelled as he paced the tile floor. "But I didn't imagine confessing while I puked up my guts."

"But you do love me."

"Yes." Finn waited, for what, he didn't know.

"Then we're good," Erin said with the same excitement she might have shown if he told her the time of day.

A few minutes later, naked and more than a little bemused by their exchange, Finn lifted his face toward the showerhead and let a sigh. He washed his hair, shaved, and stepped from the stall.

"We're good?" Finn asked the empty room. Then he realized the response was pure Erin and grinned. "Okay. I guess we're good."

CHAPTER TWENTY-FOUR

AN NFL SEASON could be measured in five parts. Starting with increments of four games each. September. October. November. December. If the team was talented, and the football gods smiled on them, then came the playoffs.

During Finn's years in the game, he tasted the postseason more than once. Three times be exact. Each ended in disappointment. Realistically, after the last play of the Super Bowl, every team but one experienced a losing season. If you didn't hoist the championship trophy, what else could be said. As with most things in life, there could only be one winner.

With only two games left in the regular season, the *Knights* were in good shape. They'd locked up the number one seed which meant the road to the big game, at least in the NFC, went through Seattle.

Unlike last year when the *Knights* were the underdog, this time all odds were on them repeating as champions. Finn was no longer a newcomer—he'd earned his stripes with a stellar season and the kind of leadership all elite teams need.

However, Finn didn't have the right to call himself a winner. Until he played in the game, won, and received a ring stamped with the word champions, he wouldn't be satisfied to simply get to the postseason. He was tired of one and done. This year, he wanted to know the sweet taste of victory instead of bitter defeat.

"Merry Christmas."

Finn grinned as Erin bounced onto the sofa, landing on his lap. She didn't bother with ornaments or reindeer figurines around her apartment—she left the over the top, a Santa in every room, decorating to her mother.

One tradition Erin embraced with enthusiasm was simple yet festive. And Finn thoroughly approved.

Eyes bright and eager, Erin held a sprig of mistletoe over Finn's head. One kiss usually led to another, then another. If they didn't end up naked, then he figured they weren't doing it right.

"Nope." Erin slipped from Finn's arms before his hands wandered beyond the outside of her clothes. "Don't have time."

"Since when?" Finn asked, reaching for her again.

"We need to talk."

Finn felt the wind whoosh from his sails. In the history of relationships, nothing good ever came from a conversation that started with, *we need to talk.*

"You're pregnant."

"I…You…" Erin sputtered.

Normally, Finn enjoyed throwing her for a loop. She was so smart and so in control most of the time, when he managed to discombobulate her, he felt a true sense of accomplishment.

Today was different. Instead of feeling smug, Finn's heart constricted. Since the moment he said I love you—under less than perfect circumstances—he hadn't waited with bated breath for Erin to reciprocate. She took longer to analyze and adjust. Confident she would get there, he waited, certain his patience, like before, would pay off.

Now, he wasn't sure. Finn didn't mean to ambush her. But since the word—pregnancy—was out there, he assumed Erin would immediately deny or confirm his suspicions. Instead, she acted as though English were a language she neither spoke nor understood.

"I'm not," Erin said. "Pregnant, that is."

"I knew what you meant." What Finn didn't know was how he felt. Relieved, or disappointed.

"Why did you think I might be?"

"Women think men are unobservant dolts, don't they?" Finn shrugged. "Okay. About some things, we are. But you and I live together. Sleep in the same bed. Make love, often. You don't think I notice when you have your period?"

"Never occurred to me that you would know one way or the other." Erin patted his head. "Impressive."

"Don't be cute," he warned.

"Sorry. You're right." Erin sobered. "I was late by a few days. And though we've been careful, no amount birth control is one hundred percent effective."

"Except abstinence, to quote my college coach."

When Finn winked, Erin smiled.

"My period started this morning, but I already knew I wasn't pregnant."

"How?" The second he asked the question, Finn felt like a fool. "You take care of pregnant ladies for a living."

"And I have access to the most accurate tests available," Erin said.

Finn took her hand.

"Are you sorry?"

"No." Erin shrugged. "Go figure. I made a big deal about wanting a baby. I thought I'd be thrilled. But the timing isn't right."

"I agree." Finn nodded and breathed easy. "In the future?"

"Maybe." She laughed. "Surprised? I guess the more I think about adoption, the more sense it makes to take care of a child who's already here."

"We could do both." Finn didn't care. If they were a family of two, he'd be happy. A child would be a bonus.

Erin nodded, then sank into a long kiss that left her breathless and him wanting more.

"Later." He moved to the other side of the sofa. "Why do we need to talk?"

"About a year ago, I decided to volunteer my services to a place where women don't get a lot of medical care. Everything got crazy. You moved to Seattle. We settled into such a lovely life. But I forgot." Erin let out a long, slow breath. "I leave the day after Christmas."

Finn didn't want to be an asshole. Erin's desire to help others less fortunate than herself was one of the things he admired about her the most. And yet, he was human. And selfish. He wanted her here. With him.

"How long will you be gone?"

When Erin didn't answer, Finn imagined the worst.

"Ten years?" With a laugh, she shook her head. "Five? A year?"

"Six months." She patted his shoulder. "A drop in the bucket compared to what you thought."

"True." Finn frowned when the implications completely sank in. "What about your promise?"

"A year ago, you were still in Chicago," Erin explained, her eyes pleading with him to understand. "The Bears won't make the playoffs this year."

"I'm in Seattle. With the Knights." Finn ran a hand through his hair and sighed. "If we go to the Super Bowl, you won't be there."

"I'm sorry." Erin placed a hand on his leg. "Do you understand why I have to go?"

"If I say no, I'm a bastard. If I say yes, a liar." Finn looked away. "Take your pick."

"We'll talk—all the time," she told him. "If I can, I'll watch the game online."

"You didn't add that you watch *if* the Knights get to the Super Bowl."

"I believe with all my heart that you will." Erin slid onto his lap. Finn hesitated, then wrapped her in his arms. "You'll win. Right?"

Finn didn't want to laugh. But somehow, in some way, Erin drew a chuckle from him.

"I won't make any promises I can't keep."

"Low blow, Finny." Erin rested her head on his shoulder and sighed. "I deserved it."

"No. You didn't. Well, maybe a little."

Finn covered her mouth with his. Sweet, filled with passion, and touched with her regret and his sadness, Finn didn't know why, but the kiss felt like an ending.

CHAPTER TWENTY-FIVE

ERIN BROKE ONE promise but kept another.

She and Finn talked often. More frequently than he imagined the day she left. Between a heavy practice schedule and the fact that she hated teary goodbyes in front of strangers, he put her in a taxi and waved as the car—and Erin disappeared from his sight.

Worry and underlying anger shadowed Finn's footsteps. But the second he hit the field, he forgot everything except the game of football. Years of sacrificing sleep for a few more hours in the gym or saying no to the piece of chocolate cake his taste buds begged him to consume finally paid off.

Finn waited too long for this moment to let anything, even a slightly battered heart, stand in his way.

The house seemed empty without her. Finn sat on the rooftop deck alone, pushing a kale salad around his plate, when his phone rang. Glancing at the screen, he almost fell out of his chair when he saw the caller ID.

"Erin?"

"You sound surprised." *She sounded wonderful.* "I said I'd call as soon as we arrived."

"The time difference threw me." Finn checked his watch. "Is it tomorrow or yesterday where you are?"

"Tomorrow." Erin laughed. "I think. Next time we talk, I'll let you know for certain."

"You'll call every day?" Finn knew he sounded clingy and desperate, but he didn't care. His woman was half a world away in a third-world country. He had the right and damn the person who said otherwise.

"If I'm at the main camp. When we go into the mountains, satellite service is almost non-existent."

"I'd say be careful," Finn said. "You'll do as you like so what's the point."

"There's my snarky Finny."

The smile in Erin's voice made his heart light and heavy at the same time. She sounded excited, which made him happy. He missed her, which sucked.

"Did you have dinner?"

"You want to waste our time talking about my eating habits?" he asked.

"No. I made Mom promise to do that," Erin told him. "Don't be surprised if she drops by now and then. Or every day. If I worry, she worries."

"A mother/daughter thing?" Finn asked.

"A Millie/Erin thing," she corrected. "Finn, I have to go. We're unloading supplies so we can get the clinic up and running tomorrow."

"I love you," Finn said.

"I—"

Finn chose to believe they were cut off accidentally—better for his peace of mind.

They didn't talk every day, but almost. Erin wanted to know about him, he wanted to know if she was safe and healthy. Her answer was always yes. Finn chose to believe her. If not, what could he do?

"Congratulations!" Erin said three weeks later. "Dr. Evans is a huge fan and keeps me up to date on the games."

Finn didn't bother to ask if Erin was tempted to watch just to see him. He knew what she would say. *You wear a helmet ninety-nine percent of the time. Why watch if I can't see your face?*

"NFC champions," Finn told her. "Next up…"

"The Super Bowl. I know," Erin said. "What about the league MVP award? When will you they give you the trophy?"

Finn grinned. Months ago, Erin decided he was a shoo-in. She didn't want to hear anything to the contrary.

"*If* I win," Finn laughed. "I should know the next time we talk."

"I don't know when I'll be able to call again. Sorry," Erin sighed. "We have a truckload of vaccines to distribute and our interpreter spread the word to the remote villages. If a woman or child makes the effort to show up, I'll treat them."

"Any idea how long you'll be gone?" Finn hated it when Erin couldn't phone him. He worried from the moment she said goodbye to the next time they said hello.

"A week. Maybe more. I'll miss your voice," she told him. "Be good and stay healthy. If some three-hundred-pound linebacker hurts a hair on your head, he'll have me to answer to."

"I'll be sure and pass along the threat."

Finn hung up and stared into the night. He knew Erin would be okay. She had to be.

FOR THE PEOPLE who considered football to be their religion, Super Bowl Sunday was the holiest of holidays. The celebration began early in the day and lasted long into the night.

If you didn't have a rooting interest in either participant, you simply enjoyed the parties, food, and atmosphere. But if your team was in the game, the day was extra special.

An emotional rollercoaster from start to finish. Cheers. Groans. Elation. Despair. Take your pick, as a fan, you experienced them all.

Players had a different perspective. From the first click of the clock to the last, they couldn't allow themselves the luxury of too many highs or lows. The important thing was to stay in the moment.

Some athletes were lucky and would return to the big game multiple times. For most, they would only be blessed with a single trip to the Super Bowl. It would be the pinnacle of their careers. A once in a lifetime experience.

As Finn suited up in the locker room, he didn't know on which side he would fall. Would he be back next year? The year after? Or would today be his one and only chance to play for the championship of the NFL?

Finn didn't want to know the answer. Instead, he planned to treat every play, every down, every quarter as though it were his last. Sports was like life. The secret was to enjoy today because no one was guaranteed a tomorrow.

Next to Finn, Levi Reynolds took his helmet from his locker and grinned.

"Back before the season started do you remember the deal we made?" the QB asked.

"I do," Finn nodded. "You, Dylan, and I lifted a beer and agreed to win the Super Bowl."

"Arrogant bastards," Levi chuckled. "Yet here we are on the precipice of doing exactly that. Guess you brought us luck, son."

"Maybe," Finn said with a cocky grin. "Or maybe we're just that good."

"Shh. Don't tempt fate." Levi winked. He watched as their teammates filed out of the locker room. "Come on. We have a game to win."

"I'll be right there," Finn said. "I just need a second."

"Take two." Levi slapped him on the back. "Then get your ass on the field."

Setting his helmet on the bench, Finn leaned against the wall. He picked up his phone and stared at the screen, willing the damn thing to ring. Nothing. Two weeks and he hadn't heard a word from Erin. Today of all days, he thought she would find a way to contact him.

Finn refused to worry. He'd been in contact with one of the doctors who worked with Erin. Everything was fine, the woman assured him. The vaccinations were going well but bringing so many people from the rural villages together took longer than anyone anticipated.

From all reports, Erin and her crew were expected back in a few days. They would talk then. But damn it, Finn wanted to hear her voice now.

"Hello, gorgeous. Did you miss me?"

Erin? Finn's head whipped around. Certain his imagination was playing tricks on him, he rubbed his eyes, expecting her image to disappear.

"I'm real." Erin laughed. She held out her arms. "Need proof?"

Finn closed the distance between them, pulled Erin into his embrace, and held on for dear life. He kissed her, releasing six weeks of pent-up passion and longing.

"I can't believe you're here," he whispered. He touched her face, tracing the line of her cheek, not the least surprised to see the slight tremor in his hand. "How?'

"We made a deal twenty years ago," Erin smiled. "Took some doing, but your boss, my friend called in some favors. Here I am. Promise kept."

"Remind me to thank Riley." Finn let out a shuddering sigh. "For the rest of my life."

"Trust me, she won't let either of us forget. But a few pairs of designer shoes and we'll be good." Erin ran a hand over Finn's face. "You let your beard grow. One of your athlete's superstitions?"

"No," Finn said. "I made up my mind not to shave until I held you in my arms again. Are you back for good?"

"Just for today," Erin told him. "I hoped you might come back with me."

"Really?" Finn frowned. "Is that possible? I don't have any medical training."

"We can always use volunteers." Erin shook her head. "We'll talk later. After the game. For now, don't move."

Finn watched as Erin hurried from the room. He breathed a sigh of relief when she returned a second later. With a mysterious smile on her lips, she walked toward him, her hands behind her back.

"Twenty years ago, you gave me something for the first time," she said. She looked around. "I know we aren't in a gymnasium, but a locker room is close enough."

"What are you doing?" Finn laughed.

Erin handed him a bouquet wrapped in a satin ribbon.

"I didn't understand back then what you wanted to say. Or all the times since. But I want you to know. My feelings are deep and strong, and forever."

"You know what they mean?" Finn asked as he looked from the flowers to Erin.

"Red tulips. A declaration of true love." Erin placed her hand on Finn's chest. Taking his hand, she placed it over her heart. "I love you, Finnegan. I'm sorry it took me so long to catch up. But I'm by your side now. If you'll take me."

"I love you." Finn brushed a kiss across Erin's lips. "But…"

"Yes?" she asked.

"I have a football game to play."

"Go." Erin laughed. She took the flowers and pushed him toward the exit.

Finn stopped and turned.

"You'll be in the stands?"

"Until the last second ticks off the clock," Erin said. "I promise."

Grinning, Finn took one last look at the woman he loved before he ran, full speed, onto the field.

VICTORY WASN'T EASY. After all, it *was* the Super Bowl. But in the end, the *Seattle Knights* came out on top. Finn caught the winning touchdown with twenty seconds left in the game.

Erin kept her promise, though whenever Finn hit the ground, covered by the oversized body of an opposing player, her eyes closed to a squint.

"Great game." Erin's father proclaimed as the Knights gathered to accept the championship trophy.

"The best," her mother agreed.

Finn flew the entire Ashmore family to the game. Cory and his wife. Erin sat beside Alan and his new fiancée, Shelly who showed off her diamond engagement ring to everyone within shouting distance.

"Finn's beard is gone," Shelly observed as the league and game's MVP removed his helmet and moved to the microphone.

"I can't believe he took the time before the game to shave," Alan said.

Erin understood the symbolism, even if her family didn't. Smiling, she kept her thoughts to herself.

"Shh," Millie told her children. "Finn's about to speak."

"I felt blessed and humbled the day I signed with Seattle. I grew up watching the *Knights*. To win a championship with my hometown team is a dream come true." Laughing with joy, Finn hefted the Lombardi trophy over his head, then handed it on to one of his teammates before continuing. "I won't thank everyone who made today possible, but I need to mention one special person. The woman I plan to spend the rest of my life with."

Gasps came from the crowd followed by loud, boisterous cheers.

"OMG." Shelly grabbed Erin's hand.

"She's been by my side, encouraged me, picked me up when I hit rock bottom." Finn's eyes lifted to the stands. "I'm here because she believed in me. I love you, Erin. With all my heart."

Erin's family turned toward her, stunned into silence. But not Shelly. She had no problem expressing herself. Arms in the air, she screamed three words.

"I knew it!"

EPILOGUE

TWO YEARS LATER

THE LIVING ROOM at the Ashmore house overflowed with friends and family there to celebrate the latest addition to the family. Erin held the baby girl as Finn looked on, smiling.

"I can't believe Marnie is three months old already." Erin laughed as the baby gurgled and burped. "Seems like only yesterday I helped bring her into the world."

"Right now, my little angel needs changing." Shelly swung her daughter into her arms. "Unless Uncle Finn would like to do the honors?"

"Thank you, but no." Finn backed away. "I might drop her."

"A football you can hold onto with no problem. But not a baby?" Erin asked her husband with a twinkle in her blue eyes.

"Footballs don't break," Finn shrugged.

"Babies are tougher than you think," Erin told him.

"Maybe." Finn wasn't convinced.

"Would you get me something to drink?" Erin asked. "I need to talk to Mom for a second."

"Sure." Finn brushed a hand over her hair. "What would you like?"

"A glass of milk." Erin smiled. "Give me five minutes? I'll meet you in the back by the old oak tree.

Finn wound his way through the crowd, stopping now and then to say hello. The topic, as always when he was around, centered on football. He understood. Even among people he'd known most of his life, his status as a member of the *Seattle Knights* made him stand out. He shook hands, posed for pictures, and tried to answer as many questions as possible.

One person who wasn't impressed by his celebrity was Erin. Never had been, never would be. They lived a normal life. Or as normal as possible for a football player and busy doctor. They laughed. And loved. And they never took for granted how lucky they were.

Twenty-plus years together as friends, then lovers, and now husband and wife. Finn looked forward to the next twenty. And the next. And the next.

"There you are," Erin said when Finn found her waiting. "I knew five minutes wasn't enough time. Too many football fans around. I'm surprised you made it to me at all."

"Nothing could keep me away." Finn set the glass of milk on the arm of a nearby lounge chair and took Erin into his arms. "I'll always find you. Every time."

"Maybe I'll be the one to find you." Erin laughed. "Women aren't the only ones who need rescuing, you know."

"My beautiful feminist." Finn gave her a lingering kiss. "You saved me more times than I can count. You still do. Every day."

When Erin took a sip from her glass, Finn frowned.

"I know your mother made her famous lemonade. Your favorite," he said. "Why did you want milk?"

"Expectant mothers need plenty of calcium," Erin told him with a smile as her hand rested on her stomach.

"You're pregnant?" Finn laughed. "We're on a waiting list to adopt."

"Any reason we can't do both?" she asked.

"Nope." Sounded good to him. "But how did this happen?"

"Finny," Erin chided. "Do I need to explain the birds and the bees to you at your age?"

"Shut up."

Finn kissed her. Love. Hope. Dreams. Everything good and right was wrapped up in this one woman. And now, their child. He couldn't imagine how life could get any better. But as Erin proved to him every day, he knew there was more to come.

Finn couldn't wait.

Turn the page to get a peek at the more books in
the **ONE PASS AWAY** series.

THE BILLIONAIRE AND THE BEAUTY
ONE PASS AWAY BOOK 5

Felicity McClain. Royce Patterson.
You met them in THE DEVIL WEARS BLUE JEANS.
Now, read their story.

He's the one man she shouldn't love. She's the one woman he can't forget.

Grab Your Copy Now

JOSHUA AND DARCY

Dark and irresistible, they call him the Devil for a reason.

The moment he touched her, held her, kissed her, she knew the dangers. She should have said no.

But unlike him, she was only human.

When Joshua McClain is hired as the Seattle Knights new head coach—a move that raises more than a few eyebrows—he's determined to prove he's not the same hot-headed troublemaker he was in his playing days. However, when he meets beautiful, exasperating, irresistible Darcy Wells, his good intentions are put to the test.

As the first woman general manager of an NFL team, Darcy knows she has a lot to prove and everything to lose. She can't afford to let herself be distracted by any man, let alone the impossibly arrogant Joshua McClain.

Joshua and Darcy have two goals. First? Return the Knights to their Super Bowl-winning glory days. Second? Do everything in their power to keep their hands off each other.

What happens when an almost reformed bad boy and a good woman with an unexpected wild side clash? Turns out there might be just enough devil in him and her to satisfy them both.

DYLAN AND EVE

Hate at first sight—with an unwanted sizzling attraction thrown in?

If they lasted a week without killing each other—or tearing each other's clothes off—it would be a miracle.

Dylan Montgomery spent his entire life cleaning up his brother's messes—and the last one is a doozy. Taking in the niece he never knew existed is a big enough chore for a dedicated bachelor—dealing with the little girl's self-appointed guardian would try the patience of a saint.

Eve Stewart learned early in life that men are born liars. From what she could tell, Dylan wasn't any different. Sure, he said all the right things, made all the right moves. And maybe his smile made her heart race in an uncomfortable way. But she didn't trust him as far as she could throw him.

With her snarky attitude and the kind of killer body that would make a saint sweat, Eve is a massive pain in Dylan's backside from day one. But he soon learns that under her tough exterior lies a vulnerable woman whose been hurt more than once by a man's lies.

Winning Eve's love is one thing. But Dylan fears earning her trust and convincing her to stay with him forever won't be as easy.

THE LAST HONEST MAN
BOOK THREE
CLICK HERE

And don't miss the originals. Gaige, Sean, and Logan. ONE PASS AWAY

Logan's story: **AFTER THE RAIN: CLICK HERE**

Sean's story: **AFTER ALL THESE YEARS: CLICK HERE**

Gaige's story: **AFTER THE FIRE: CLICK HERE**

And catch up with the **ONE PASS AWAY** boys in the spin-off series, **ONE STRIKE AWAY**.

Four sexy baseball players heat up the diamond. Four women, they can't resist. Grab your copy now.

CLICK HERE

AUDIOBOOKS

ONE PASS AWAY SERIES

After the Rain – *click here*

After All These Years – *click here*

After the Fire - *click here*

HOLLYWOOD LEGENDS SERIES

Dreaming with a Broken Heart – *click here*

Dreaming with My Eyes Wide Open - *click here*

Dreaming of Your Love - *click here*

Dreaming Again - *click here*

HARPER FALLS SERIES

If I Loved You – *click here*

If Tomorrow Never Comes – *click here*

If You Only Knew – *click here*

If I Had You – *click here*

THE SISTERS QUARTET

One Way or Another - *click here*

Mary J. Williams

MORE BOOKS BY MARY J. WILLIAMS

Harper Falls
If I Loved You

If Tomorrow Never Comes

If You Only Knew

If I Had You (Christmas in Harper Falls)

Hollywood Legends
Dreaming with a Broken Heart

Dreaming with My Eyes Wide Open

Dreaming of Your Love

Dreaming Again

Dreaming of a White Christmas

(Caleb and Callie's story)

One Pass Away
After the Rain

After All These Years

After the Fire

Hart of Rock and Roll
Flowers on the Wall

Mary J. Williams

The Heartbreak Kid

<u>Almost Everything</u>

<u>Almost Home</u>

<u>Almost Like Being in Love (A Rock & Roll Forever Christmas)</u>

<u>One Pass Away—A New Season</u>

<u>The Devil Wears Blue Jeans</u>

<u>The Back-Up Plan</u>

<u>The Last Honest Man</u>

ABOUT THE AUTHOR

Writing isn't easy. But I love every second. A blank screen isn't the enemy. It is an opportunity to create new friends and take them on amazing adventures and life-changing journeys. I feel blessed to spend my days weaving tales that are unique—because I made them.

Billionaires. Songwriters. Artists. Actors. Directors. Stuntmen. Football players. They fill the pages becoming dear friends I hope you will want to revisit again and again.

Thank you for jumping into my books and coming along for the journey

HOW TO GET IN TOUCH

Please visit me at these sites, sign up for my newsletter, or leave a message.

Bookbub
Newsletter
Facebook
Twitter
Pinterest
Instagram
Goodreads

Made in the USA
Monee, IL
13 January 2022

88857944R00125